CULTURAL DIFFERENCES

CULTURAL
Differences

A SMALL TOWN LESBIAN ROMANCE

LOVE IN DOWNEAST MAINE, BOOK 1

ARYA COLLINS

SAPPHIROM PRESS

ONE

AFTER ALMOST A year of telling herself she wasn't ready for another relationship, Lauren had to admit her plan was working pretty well. Too well, actually.

The summer had been rough. The steady stream of tourists at Great Expectations, the bookstore where she worked, had brought a few opportunities for light flirting, which was all she was prepared to do at the time. Now, it was the final weekend before classes started at the University of Maine campus across the river, on the southeast side of town. Lauren had lived in Zachary most of her life, and the pattern of tourist traffic was as familiar as the spectacular, changing colors that brought a fresh surge of visitors in the fall. In a few weeks, the tourist stream would diminish to a trickle and then dry up once the snow started falling.

Maybe it was the change of seasons, but Lauren was starting to realize she wanted something more than flirting with women she would never see again.

Of course, there were always the locals. Among the five thousand or so permanent residents of Zachary—the city's population nearly doubled during the academic year—Lauren figured she probably knew all two lesbians. She was one. As for Kelly...well, that was a road she wasn't prepared to travel again.

She sighed as she moved a stack of books off the counter. She was more likely to meet someone on campus. Unfortunately for Lauren, being among students could only remind her of another, larger University of Maine campus, where her own college days had come to an abrupt end.

"Big plans for the weekend?" Jen, her boss and the owner of Great Expectations bustled by, carrying a carton of paperbacks.

"Not really." Lauren made room for her behind the counter, and Jen dumped the box on the floor with a thud, raising a small cloud of dust. "I've been meaning to do a binge-watching session for *Quantico*. I have the whole last season in my streaming queue, but I haven't had a chance to watch all the episodes yet."

Jen laughed. She was one of the two people who knew Lauren's innermost secrets—things that even Lauren's mother didn't know. The other was Lauren's childhood friend, Josh Bennett. Jen pushed back her ginger curls with one hand and squeezed Lauren's shoulder with the other. "You won't be here Sunday, so make the most of it. I've never watched that show. You must really like it."

"It's not the show itself, although I admit they do have good writers. It's...well, I've had a crush on the lead actress ever since the first episode." Lauren walked over to the counter to help a customer check out. The woman, about the age of Lauren's mother, was carrying a stack of romance novels, with the obligatory bare-chested alpha male on the covers.

Lauren glanced up at the customer and gave her a huge smile as she bagged the books. "I'm sure you'll enjoy them. They look really hot. Thanks for shopping with us."

The woman's eyes opened wide, and she mumbled something incoherent, grabbed the bag, and headed for the door. Lauren had to control her urge to laugh. Didn't the poor woman know she could buy all those books online and have them shipped to her home? Alternatively, she could enjoy the privacy of an e-reader, and not have giddy bookstore workers comment on her reading habits. Still, it was customers like her who kept Great Expectations in business. On most days, Lauren enjoyed her job. There was something calming about being surrounded by books, and she liked to believe that it helped fuel her own hesitant and irregular attempts at writing a novel. Although she'd published a few short stories in magazines when she was in college, Lauren had come to realize that writing a novel was quite a different story—literally. When she started out, she had no idea how much effort she'd need to put into planning her urban fantasy series. Lauren envied those writers who could just sit down and start writing, without doing any planning at all, but her brain wasn't wired that way. She'd already done extensive world building, plotting, and outlining before she even made it to chapter one. She told herself it would all pay off some day. If not monetarily, at least in the satisfaction of having completed her first novel.

Jen drew Lauren out of her reverie, brushing past to help another customer, and Lauren wandered back into the stacks. It was still early, for a Friday, but there were quite a few people browsing the shelves. Most of them appeared to be students, some with parents in tow, apparently taking a break during move-in weekend to visit the smattering of downtown businesses. Zachary didn't boast much of a downtown, at least compared to Orono and its close neighbor Bangor, which was the only other place Lauren had lived. The bookstore occupied a prime location at the corner of Bluebird Avenue and Main Street. Together with Fleischmann's Bakery next door, it drew most of the attention. A few other local businesses lined Main Street in either direction, and Jen was proud of the fact that Zachary had no chain restaurants or big box stores. While Lauren had always appreciated the charm of downtown Zachary, she did occasionally miss the variety of shopping options available in Bangor.

Lauren braced herself for the uptick in traffic that would follow when it got closer to noon. After about an hour of ushering customers through the stacks in search of books they knew they wanted but couldn't quite describe, while Jen handled the register, she and Jen swapped duties. Great Expectations was small enough that the two of them could handle the work during the off season with part-time help. Although it had been a while since Jen had discussed the financials with her, Lauren sometimes wondered how the store had survived this long. She'd been working there for almost three years now and, even in that time, she'd noticed that the sales volume had declined each year, especially through the fall and winter.

At noon, their part-time assistant Sonia would arrive, and that would help Lauren considerably. She really liked Sonia, who was a sophomore at the university. Regretfully, Lauren recalled this was going to be Sonia's last weekend at the store. From what Lauren could tell, Sonia had a full class load planned for the fall semester, and then some. Lauren was going to miss her.

She didn't like admitting it to herself, but Lauren knew she'd have to consider a career beyond the bookstore at some point, as her mother kept reminding her. Unfortunately, as her mother also reminded her, the key to a more lucrative career was a college degree. For the moment, Lauren was happy where she was. It was comfortable, and she wasn't ready to move out beyond her comfort zone just yet.

"Excuse me, miss, could you help me find a cookbook? I'm particularly interested in seafood recipes."

Lauren's head whipped around. "Of course." As she led the woman back through the stacks, Lauren wondered why her customer hadn't searched one of the many recipe sites online, where she could most likely find exactly what she wanted. The store sold very few cookbooks. Still, a customer was a customer. Leaving the woman to browse through the solitary shelf of cookbooks, Lauren returned to the counter.

The bell above the door sounded, and a young blonde woman caught Lauren's eye. Her shorts hugged her hips, which tapered into long, tanned legs. Lauren's gaze traveled upward to the woman's V-necked white T shirt, which displayed her cleavage to perfection. Lauren turned her smile up to maximum wattage, but her interest soon faded when a guy walked in behind the blonde and placed a hand on her hips. The blonde giggled and smacked his hand away.

With a sigh, Lauren turned back to the counter. It was going to be a long day.

TWO

NALINI RIPPED OPEN the tape on a box, the sound shattering the silence in the close confines of her graduate dorm room. At first, the silence had been welcome, but now it was adding to her unease at being alone in a strange place. For a moment, she wished she had taken her aunt and uncle up on their offer to extend their stay in Zachary through the weekend. It had been less than a day since they'd left, and she missed them already.

When Nalini had disclosed her plan a few months earlier to take a Greyhound bus up the coast to Zachary, they'd reacted as if Nalini had just plunged a knife into their chests.

"Nonsense!" Her aunt had crossed her arms and glared at Nalini. "Your uncle and I won't hear of it. We're your family, and we're going to help you get settled in."

After they'd made it through the six-hour drive on Friday with one stop, Nalini had felt a twinge of guilt at the thought of them turning back around and returning the same day. Her uncle had mentioned finding a motel so they could remain in Zachary longer. Instead, Nalini had convinced them to drive back to Boston as originally planned, so they'd miss most of the weekend traffic.

Now, she lay sprawled out on her bed in the sparsely furnished room, with a stack of boxes still unpacked. The first item she'd retrieved from the boxes soon after they'd unloaded her uncle's car Friday afternoon had been the Bluetooth speaker system for her iPhone.

Music always helped her feel better. She turned up the volume and let the husky, seductive tones of Lana del Rey wash over her as she closed her eyes. Somehow, it was strange to feel homesick for a city in which she'd only lived four years, considering she'd spent the rest of her life more than seven thousand miles away.

And yet, Nalini realized, it wasn't just Wellesley College she missed. It wasn't just a place. It was an experience, and a large part of that experience included her friends. They'd all promised to keep in touch, but Nalini knew the realities of their new lives would soon take over, and she'd be lucky if they even exchanged holiday greetings in a few years.

Well, it was time to make new friends...

Nalini's stomach growled loud enough to be heard over the music. She realized she hadn't eaten anything since grabbing a coffee and candy bar from the vending machine after waking up early that morning. With a sigh, she rolled off the bed, hit the power button on the stereo, and slipped her phone back into the pocket of her shorts.

Although each floor of Jorgensen Hall had its own kitchenette—a feature highlighted in one of the numerous brochures she'd received in her welcome packet—there was only one problem. The mini fridge in Nalini's room was empty, and the dining halls scattered across the campus weren't open yet. It looked like she'd need to make another trip to the vending machine.

As Nalini headed down the hallway, the distinctive beep of the microwave told her she no longer had the place to herself. The man at the microwave turned and smiled as she walked in.

"Haven't seen you before. You must be new." He extended a hand. "I'm Paul." The corners of his eyes crinkled as he shook her hand, squeezing her fingers with a little more pressure than she'd expected.

"Nalini. And yes, I arrived yesterday." She retrieved her hand. "How about you?"

"This is my third year here. I'm in the physics department, doing my doctoral research in the Murray lab."

"Third year? But I thought—"

"—most students escape graduate housing after their first year, if they use it at all. Yes, that's true enough." The microwave beeped again, but Paul made no move to open the door. "Some of us are strange that way, though. Think about it. Who wouldn't pass up a chance to live in the lap of luxury, with an entire floor of other misfits? Why, we even have our own bathrooms. It's practically The Press Hotel."

Nalini raised her eyebrows. "I don't know where that is, but it sounds fancy." The aroma of melted cheese made her stomach growl again, and her cheeks grew warm. "Sorry. I've been so busy unpacking that I forgot to eat." She glanced at the vending machines.

Paul opened the microwave door. "You know, if you like microwave pizza, you're welcome to have this one. I have a few more in the freezer. Just stocked up last night."

Nalini giggled as her stomach expressed its frustration more intently this time. "Thanks, that's very generous of you. I'm a vegetarian, though, so I should probably try to head into town and see what I can find there."

He sat the pizza down on a table. "This one's just cheese. Actually, that's all I have at the moment. Do you eat cheese?"

"Yes, I do." The pizza did look tempting, certainly more so than the bag of chips she'd planned on getting. "If it's not too much trouble..."

"No trouble at all." He disappeared behind the door of the freezer that sat next to the microwave, eventually emerging with another orange box. After he ripped it open and set it in the microwave, Paul turned back to Nalini. "Would you like a soda? I'm going to grab one for myself."

She grinned. "As long as you're buying, I'll take a diet, please. Are you this nice to all the new grad students?"

He chuckled as he headed for the soda machine. "Only the pretty ones."

Nalini shook her head and blew on the pizza, which was still steaming. She tore off a prescored slice and had devoured most of it by the time Paul returned, ignoring the momentary twinge of pain as molten cheese seared the roof of her mouth.

He settled into a chair across from her. "It's not much, I know, but when you're hungry..."

"It's perfect, and thanks again. I owe you one. I survived on cafeteria food for four years at Wellesley, although they did have quite a few vegetarian options. Frozen dinners are just about the only thing I can cook, though."

"Wellesley? How come you're here and not somewhere in Boston?"

"I made the mistake of applying to the graduate program at Harvard, after my parents insisted. To be honest, I'd always wanted to attend a smaller school, and this is one of the few marine biology graduate programs on the east coast." She wiped her mouth with a napkin, then attacked another slice.

"Were your parents disappointed you didn't get into Harvard?" Paul pushed his chair back and walked over to the microwave. He returned with his pizza and sat next to her.

"To put it mildly, yes. They blamed my undergraduate grades on partying too much in my senior year. Honestly, I didn't think my grades were that bad."

"Did you? Party all year, I mean."

She affected a pout. "I'll have you know I was a very studious girl. Well, most of the time."

As Nalini watched with fascination, Paul proceeded to fold his entire single-serving pizza in half and then took a large bite from one end.

"That's a...very interesting way to eat a pizza." She suppressed a giggle.

"You should try it some time." His voice was muffled, interrupted by vigorous chewing. "Less mess on the fingers."

"So, what about you? How did you end up here?"

Paul waited until he'd finished chewing to respond. "I grew up in Portland. Lived there all my life, actually. I really got into an obscure area of superstring theory when I took an advanced physics class, and I knew I wanted to pursue graduate studies. I never expected to find someone doing that type of research here, though. It's a small graduate program, compared to the main campus at Orono but well, here I am."

"I have to admit I didn't do too well in my undergrad physics classes." Nalini reached for the remaining slice of pizza in front of her. "I did consider a chemistry major for a while, but biology fascinated me. I was one of those weird kids who was interested in all kinds of life forms. Bugs, worms, birds, whatever I could observe. I can't even remember the number of stray dogs that used to follow me home from school."

They continued discussing their career paths for a while, and Paul's sense of humor and irreverent attitude toward higher education put Nalini increasingly at ease. Before she realized it, a whole hour had passed. Reluctantly, she rose from the table and scooped up the grease-stained cardboard remnants of their meals.

As she discarded them, she thanked Paul again.

"No worries," he said with a grin. "You can buy me dinner some time, if you insist on paying me back."

Nalini laughed. She wondered if Paul would still be this welcoming if he'd discovered she had absolutely no interest in him other than as a friend.

When Nalini finished unpacking the last box later that afternoon, she celebrated by buying herself another soda from the vending machine. This time, the kitchenette was deserted. Back in her room, she arranged and rearranged her personal possessions until she achieved an effect that came close to the familiar clutter of her room at Wellesley. When she was done, she decided to check out the town and find a store where she could stock up on some convenience foods.

She checked a map on her phone to get a sense of her bearings. She'd only caught a glimpse of the small downtown neighborhood when her aunt and uncle had driven through it the day before. It looked like an easy, fifteen-minute walk from campus, across the river, to the main street that ran through downtown Zachary. The only issue was that she'd have to use the bridge over the river. Back at Wellesley, she'd learned the technical term for a fear of bridges: gephyrophobia. She was fairly sure she wasn't a full-blown gephyrophobiac, but the prospect still made her a bit uneasy. She took a deep breath. She'd cross that bridge when she came to it, quite literally.

She was about to put her phone away when it rang.

"Hi, mom." Nalini settled back on her bed. "Isn't it late for you there? It must be past midnight."

"We were out late at your Uncle Vinod's place," her mother replied. "You know how it is when your father and Vinod start drinking. Actually, I wanted to call you yesterday to see how the move went, but I forgot how to calculate the time difference again."

"There's an app for that," Nalini said, suppressing a sigh. "It's already on your phone."

"You know I don't like these smartphone things. Your father made me use this new one, because of his international calling plan and all that nonsense, but I still prefer my old landline phone."

"Don't worry, mom, I'm sure you'll figure it out. Just ask Sanjeev to help you. How's he doing, by the way?"

"Your cousin is fine. He's hoping to get a promotion next month. But I didn't call to chit-chat."

"Oh?" Nalini bit back a retort. She knew what was coming next.

"Nalu...have you thought about what we discussed before you left Boston? The parents have contacted me again, and they're anxious to make arrangements—"

"I'm not going to get married now, mom. Especially to some guy I met only once as a child. I haven't changed my mind over the past week. I'm not likely to change it for...oh, I don't know...forever!"

Her mother made a disapproving cluck. "Nalu, you're not getting any younger. We have to think about these things. After all, we're your parents. Your father told me you'd be obstinate about this, but it's my duty—"

"I don't want to discuss this further. Goodbye."

Nalini ended the call. A powerful urge to fling her iPhone across the room overcame her, and it was only her love of the diminutive device that kept her from acting on it.

When the phone rang again, a few moments later, she let the call go through to voicemail without bothering to check the screen. Muttering to herself, she walked out the door. All of a sudden, her dorm room seemed more confining than ever.

THREE

AROUND TWO IN the afternoon, things slowed down again at the bookstore, and Lauren reached under the counter for the book she was reading. One of the perks of working at Great Expectations was the employee discount, and she had no shortage of reading material. She had somewhat eclectic tastes that ranged from the classics to young adult fantasy, and she'd just started the first book of Brandon Sanderson's *Reckoners* series. She had barely got past a few pages when the brass bell attached to the door jingled. She looked up and froze.

It couldn't be. Why would Priyanka Chopra be visiting Zachary, of all places? The young woman who stepped inside must have noticed Lauren staring, for she paused and favored Lauren with a shy smile. Lauren couldn't stop staring, drinking in every little detail, from the waves of glossy black hair that tumbled carelessly down to her shoulders, to the long lashes that fluttered over her warm brown eyes. Lauren's gaze lingered on the woman's extremely kissable, candy-pink lips. She took several deep breaths, trying to calm herself. It had to be a dream. Any moment now, she'd wake up and find herself alone in bed. She blinked and pinched her arm hard, but the woman was still there.

It wasn't Priyanka Chopra, of course. Now that the initial shock was fading, Lauren could discern small differences that only a true PC fan would notice. With another quick smile that made

Lauren's pulse race, the gorgeous stranger turned and disappeared among the stacks.

Lauren glanced around the store and spotted Jen fussing with a display in what they called the "power aisle"—the one with the most popular bestsellers arranged for maximum effect. She waited until Jen turned around, then caught her eye and made a series of convoluted gestures.

Finally, Jen straightened up and walked over. "What's up? Are you okay? You look a little frazzled. Do you need to take your break?"

"I'm fine." Lauren took another deep breath. "I was just wondering if you could cover the counter for a bit. I...um...I have to go help a customer."

Jen raised her eyebrows, her eyes suggesting she wanted to ask more, but she nodded. It was one of the things Lauren loved about her. Jen could practically read Lauren's mind at times.

After a quick glance around the rest of the store, Lauren wandered over to the stacks and sauntered past the end displays, doing her best helpful-bookstore-employee impression. When she got to the far end of the room, Lauren spotted the woman browsing through the literary fiction shelves. Now that Lauren could get a better look, she reluctantly confirmed that her initial wild suspicions about the stranger's identity were groundless. Although her bronze, flawless complexion was the same shade as Lauren's crush, the woman's nose was longer and straighter than PC's, and her ears seemed a bit smaller and more delicate, in proportion to the rest of her face.

Sucking in a deep breath, Lauren shouldered her way into the narrow aisle. The woman looked up as Lauren approached, and her luscious lips parted slightly.

Lauren gulped and cleared her throat. "Can I help you with anything?"

"Actually, yes. I was looking for Jhumpa Lahiri's last novel. Not the Italian book, but the one she published about six or seven years ago. It doesn't appear to be on the shelf." Even her voice sounded like PC's, just a bit huskier.

"*The Lowland*?" In contrast, Lauren's voice came out as a squeak. "It should be here." She scanned the shelf but, sure enough, there were no copies left. "I've read it, by the way. It's really good, but I like her short stories better."

The woman's eyes lit up. "You like Jhumpa Lahiri?"

"I do." Lauren smiled back, her eyes lingering on those lips. *Kiss her now*, a crazy little voice in the back of Lauren's head said. What was happening to her? "I've read all her books. Well, except for the new Italian one you mentioned. And the weird one about book jackets. That was also in Italian, if I recall correctly."

The woman's smile grew broader, and dimples appeared in her cheeks. "Yeah, I haven't read the Italian ones either." She had a lilting accent that Lauren recognized from her PC obsession, but there was a hint of Boston in there as well. "I'm Nalini, by the way."

Lauren smiled and held out a hand. "I'm Lauren." Nalini's hand was warm and soft in hers, and Lauren held it a smidgen longer than she'd intended before letting it drop. Her cheeks flushed as she gestured to the shelf. "We must have run out of copies. Let me go check our inventory, and I'll be right back. Don't go away."

This time, Nalini laughed. The sound made Lauren's stomach clench up with the urge, once again, to plant a kiss on those enticing lips. Nalini flipped her hair back. "I promise. I'll stay right here."

The last time Lauren fell for a straight woman, it hadn't turned out so well. Hadn't she learned anything from her previous disasters? She walked to the back of the store, into the glorified closet that served as Jen's office. She typed in the book, clicked the search button, and sighed. Zero copies.

Like most customers, Lauren figured Nalini would probably just go home and order it online. She walked back, shaking her head.

"I'm sorry, we don't have any in stock. If you like, I can move up our next order. We could have it for you by the middle of next week." She held her breath.

"That would be great." Nalini waved a book that she'd been holding. "I have this one for now, anyway. Let me give you my information."

"I can take it when I check you out...I mean, at the checkout." Lauren's cheeks flamed again. To cover up her blunder, Lauren dived in further. "Did anyone ever tell you that you look—"

"—like Priyanka Chopra?" Once again, Nalini laughed, sending a delicious shiver down Lauren's spine. "Yes, I've heard that a few times. To be honest, a lot of Indian women in America probably do, though." Her eyes danced with laughter as she gave Lauren another dazzling smile.

Lauren could spend all day staring into those eyes. "Are you just visiting our fine town in the middle of nowhere?"

Nalini giggled. "Not exactly. I just moved here. I'm starting graduate school at the university."

Lauren's stomach did a weird flip. "That's great. Welcome to Zachary, home of absolutely nothing. Except the university, I guess."

"Thank you." Nalini's cheeks dimpled again. "It is a bit remote, isn't it? Especially compared to Boston, where my aunt and uncle live. But I love what I've seen so far. I think a small town like this will be a nice change. Actually, Wellesley felt like living in a bubble at times, but we could always escape to Boston."

It was then that Lauren noticed Nalini's T-shirt. She'd been too busy checking out Nalini's breasts for the logo to register. Quickly, Lauren looked back up into Nalini's eyes again. "I've only been to Boston a few times, but I liked it there. This is really going to be something of a culture shock for you, I'm afraid."

Lauren led the way out of the stacks. Jen gave Lauren a curious look but said nothing as she yielded her spot at the register to Lauren. "I know there's not much to see around here, but if you need someone to show you around town, let me know. I'd be happy to help. I'm working till we close tonight, but I have tomorrow off."

Nalini squeezed Lauren's hand, and Lauren had to bite her lip to stop herself from potentially losing a sale by pulling her prospective customer into her arms.

"Thank you," Nalini said. "I'd like that. I don't have a car, so I'm limited to what's within walking distance. Fortunately, I enjoy walking, at least when the weather's as nice as it is today."

Lauren scanned Nalini's book. It was a new release by Kunal Basu, an author she had yet to read. She rang up the sale, wrote her cell phone number on one of the store's business cards, and slipped it into the book. After she had entered Nalini's information, double-checking it, she promised to call Nalini as soon as the Jhumpa Lahiri book arrived.

"Thanks," Nalini said again. "You'll probably hear from me tomorrow. I'll text you."

As Nalini walked out the door, Lauren's gaze was drawn to her perfect ass, hugged tight by her faded jean shorts. There was a bright side to the current heat wave, after all.

Once again, Lauren told herself, this was definitely not a good idea. She had to stop drooling over her customers. Nalini had merely been friendly, nothing more.

"So, what was all that about?" Jen grabbed Lauren's elbow, jolting her out of her Nalini-induced trance, and Lauren jumped.

"Priyanka Chopra."

Jen frowned. "Who?"

"PC. *Quantico?* Oh, that's right. I forgot you haven't watched the show."

Jen's eyes bored into Lauren's. "Be careful, Lauren." She put her hand on Lauren's shoulder.

"I know." Lauren had told Jen most of what had happened a couple of years ago, when she'd developed an infatuation with her friend Jasmine, who wasn't into women. She'd ended up ruining a perfectly good friendship. Then, of course, she'd jumped right into another relationship with Kelly. It was glorious while it lasted, until Lauren discovered Kelly wasn't really over her ex-girlfriend and had slept with her while Kelly and Lauren were together. Fortunately, Kelly had moved to Portland soon after the breakup, so Lauren didn't have to worry about running into her at the grocery store.

Jen massaged Lauren's shoulder, and she relaxed. "It's okay, Jen," she said, more to convince herself than anything else. "She's new in town, and I told her I'd help her get adjusted. Besides, she's way out of my league, even if she is gay by some miracle. A marine biology graduate student and a college dropout. Yeah, that would work."

"You're too hard on yourself sometimes." Jen moved away as a customer approached. "I just don't want you to get hurt, that's all."

It was good advice, and it comforted Lauren to know that Jen cared enough to give it. Regrettably, Lauren had a spectacularly bad track record when it came to taking advice, from Jen or anyone else.

FOUR

THE WALK BACK to campus seemed longer than before, and Nalini almost wished she had bought a car when she was at Wellesley. She did have a driver's license, thanks to her uncle's encouragement, although she'd never driven when she lived in Mumbai.

"If you can drive in Boston, you can drive anywhere in the world," he'd said. After several harrowing experiences and a near miss while entering a roundabout, her confidence had taken a considerable hit. And yet, she'd managed to survive the classes at the driving school and still treasured the little piece of plastic that she kept in her purse.

When she was accepted to graduate school at Zachary, she'd considered asking her uncle to cosign a loan so she could buy a used car, but she never quite got up the nerve to ask him. Besides, she didn't want to have car payments eat up what remained of the meager stipend from her teaching assistantship, despite the money her parents transferred into her bank account on a regular basis to meet her living expenses. She had learned that their generosity invariably came with strings attached.

At least the weather was perfect for a walk. As she rearranged the bags in her hands, Nalini smiled. She had already made a friend in Zachary, besides Paul. Lauren was adorable. Even though they'd barely spent fifteen minutes in conversation, Nalini felt a distinct connection, as if they'd known each other for years. She was definitely looking forward to seeing Lauren again.

Although she'd made extensive use of it when moving in, Nalini felt somewhat guilty about taking the building's solitary elevator up to the third floor. She promised herself she'd take the stairs at every opportunity from now on. When the polished steel doors opened and she got out, she spotted Paul waving to her from the other end of the hallway.

"Stocking up your fridge?" He glanced at the bags she was holding.

She grinned. "Just junk food, mostly."

Paul spread his hands. "Hey, grad students have been surviving on junk food for centuries. Nothing wrong with that. Are you doing anything tonight?"

Nalini paused for a moment. "Not really. I'm just going to hang out here and watch TV, or I might catch up with my book."

"I'm on my way to the lab now, but how about going out for a drink later? There's a bar close by that's pretty popular with grad students. I'd hate for you to be all alone on your first Saturday night in Zachary."

Nalini had resigned herself to the expectation that graduate students worked seven days a week, so Paul's admission that he was heading into the lab didn't surprise her. Once she chose her advisor, she'd be doing the same thing—spending her life with her nose buried in her research projects. Still, she had two semesters before she had to make that decision. Hanging out at a bar didn't sound too bad, even if she suspected that Paul's motives weren't strictly based on welcoming a new student to campus.

"You *are* old enough to drink, right?" He tilted his head, grinning.

"Do I look l like a kid, or are you just trying to make me feel good?" Nalini returned his grin. "Actually, I turned twenty-one earlier this year. A drink sounds good."

"Great!" Paul gave her a thumbs-up. "I'll meet you outside at seven."

When she got back to her room, Nalini wondered if she'd made a mistake in accepting Paul's invitation. Unless she was completely misreading his intentions, he seemed to have more than just a casual interest in her life. She sighed. Some instinct had made her like Paul already, but she'd have to set him straight and the sooner, the better.

True to his word, Paul was seated on the steps in front of the double doors when Nalini wandered outside just after seven. A faint vestigial glow was all that was left of the sun, and the unseasonal warmth of the day had faded. Nalini had grabbed a light jacket before leaving her room. Paul was wearing a U of M hooded sweatshirt, and Nalini resolved to get one for herself as soon as she had the chance. She still had a substantial collection of Wellesley gear, but she didn't quite feel right wearing it on campus.

As Paul had promised, the walk to Clive's Tavern was a short one. Lauren had mentioned another bar on the east side of town, Cooper's Tavern, that had a more rustic atmosphere. They had live music on the weekends and Nalini's ears had perked up when Lauren said she hung out there with her friend Josh fairly regularly. A part of her had, irrationally, hoped that Lauren might be interested in her as more than a friend, but it sounded as if Lauren and Josh were pretty close. Still, she'd hoped Lauren would extend an invitation for Nalini to join them and was more than a little disappointed when it appeared that none was forthcoming.

In contrast to the mental picture Nalini had formed of Cooper's, Clive's looked like a recent addition to Zachary.

"They opened six or seven years ago, I think," Paul said, in response to her question. "It's a convenient location for students, especially if you don't have a car and don't want to hike over to Cooper's."

They ordered their drinks at the bar, Nalini choosing a usual strawberry margarita and Paul picking a draft beer from the Zachary River Brewing Company. Nalini glanced around the bar and thought she spotted a couple of familiar faces from the dorm but nobody that she knew. They took their drinks to a table.

Paul took a long sip of his beer and sighed in appreciation. "You're not a beer drinker, I take it?"

Nalini waved a hand. "Not really. I mean, I liked Indian beer when I was a kid, but it wasn't my drink of choice."

Paul's eyes grew wide. "You drank beer as a kid?"

She shrugged. "Alcohol wasn't a big deal in our family. I didn't drink the whole bottle, of course, but a lot of parents let their kids have a few sips at parties or family gatherings. After I moved here, I realized how unusual that was."

Paul raised his glass. "To Indian parents."

"You might not say that about my parents if you knew them." Nalini smiled and clinked her glass against his. "They're very conservative about most other things. Like religion and...well, sexual identity."

Paul raised an eyebrow, and Nalini took a deep breath before plunging in. "For example, they still have no idea that their dear daughter is a lesbian." She chuckled when Paul almost did a classic spit-take. "Sorry. I didn't mean to spring it on you like that."

"I should have known," he said, after he'd recovered. "That's why you didn't succumb to my irresistible charm as soon as we met."

Nalini patted his hand. "I'm glad you're taking it so well."

"Have you tried talking to them about it?"

"Trust me, it wouldn't end well. Yes, things are changing in India, slowly. However, my parents have been stuck in the past for as long as I can remember. I do miss them, but it was actually something of a relief when I got my acceptance letter from Wellesley. I saw it as an opportunity to start my life over." She bowed her head, thinking of the last phone conversation with her mother. In some ways, she hadn't really escaped her parents' influence at all.

"I know this is none of my business, so feel free to slap me down." Paul lifted his glass and took another long sip. "Do you ever plan to tell them?"

She sighed. "I don't know. They've arranged a marriage for me to some guy I don't even know, so I guess I'll have to figure it out at some point."

He nodded. "I hope everything works out. Well, let's talk of more pleasant things. Like supersymmetry between bosons and fermions, for example."

Nalini laughed. "You really do know how to make a girl feel special, Paul. I'm glad you brought me here. It definitely beats moping alone in my room."

Despite Paul's earnest attempts to initiate her into the mysteries of superstring theory, Nalini did begin to enjoy her night out. She managed to steer the conversation toward more familiar topics, like books and music. To her surprise, it was past midnight when they returned to Jorgensen Hall.

Back in her room, Nalini reflected on the question Paul had asked about her parents. She'd certainly considered coming out to her parents on a few occasions. Maybe now that she was starting a new phase of her career, it would be the right time. Then again, she'd told herself the same thing in her first semester at Wellesley, and over four years had gone by without her finding the courage to raise the issue.

Before she settled into bed that night, she checked her phone and deleted the voicemail from her mother without bothering to play it. Then she reached for the book that sat on her nightstand and opened it. A business card fell out and fluttered to the floor.

Nalini picked it up. Her heart beat just a little faster as she turned the card over and looked at the number neatly handwritten on the back. Maybe tomorrow would be an even better day.

FIVE

LAUREN COULD HAVE hugged Sonia when she showed up for her shift Saturday afternoon. Thanks to Sonia working the full weekend, Lauren was able to take Sunday off. The bookstore was open seven days a week during the tourist season. Although hours were reduced during the off season, Jen had been discussing staying open longer, as some of the other downtown businesses were doing.

"I'm going to miss this place," Sonia said, as she squeezed past Lauren with an armload of books.

"We're going to miss you, too. Are you sure you won't change your mind about working here during the semester?"

Sonia sighed as she began shelving the books. "I'd love to if I could. I could definitely use the money, but I have a full course load, and there's just no way I could make it work. I'm hoping to graduate next spring."

Graduation was something Lauren had looked forward to when she started college. Now, it was just an elusive dream. She wondered what Nalini would think about her lack of a college education. For some reason, Nalini's opinion was suddenly important to Lauren. It was silly, Lauren knew, because they had only just met. And yet, Lauren couldn't stop thinking about Nalini's warm brown eyes and the cute dimples in her cheeks when she smiled.

After Nalini had left, the store was filled with a steady stream of customers, most likely visitors to campus who were exploring the downtown area. It helped keep Lauren's mind off Nalini, to some extent. Yet, like a starry-eyed schoolgirl, she kept listening for that buzz from her phone that signaled an incoming text. She'd hoped that Nalini would find an excuse to contact her, even though they hadn't made any plans until Sunday. Maybe, just maybe, Nalini was interested in a little more than a tour guide.

Lauren shook her head. This was ridiculous. She really needed to get a grip.

When Lauren took her break, she considered texting Nalini for a moment. Instead, she managed to distract herself with some light flirtation. Her first victim was a gorgeous redhead who was a freshman at the university. After chatting with Lauren for a few minutes, though, the redhead soon rejoined a giggling group of her friends, and they left the store without buying anything.

Next, Lauren spotted an older woman browsing the store's admittedly thin lesbian romance section. Lauren didn't have a thing for older women, although there was a time in the past where she would have jumped into bed with any woman who was able and willing. Something about the customer caught Lauren's attention.

The woman must have noticed it, too, because her gaze traveled up and down Lauren's body, making Lauren's cheeks flush.

"Do you have any...um...personal recommendations?" she asked, laying a hand on Lauren's shoulder. "I'm only in town for the weekend, and I wanted a quickie. A quick read, I mean." Her eyes bored into Lauren's, and her tongue traced a slow, sensuous path across her lower lip.

Fighting back the urge to respond the way her body was dictating, Lauren tried to maintain a calm, professional air. "If you like contemporary romance, try the *New Beginnings* series by Meredith Winters. I have to admit, though, that most of my favorite lesbian romance authors are self-published. Unfortunately, we

don't typically carry self-published books in the store. I'm hoping
that will change soon."

"Thank you." The words came out as a breathy whisper, and
the woman trailed her fingers down Lauren's arm. With a su-
preme effort, Lauren pulled her eyes away from the tanned skin
exposed by the woman's tank top.

It would be easy. The woman was sending off signals that Lauren would have picked up a mile away. A mindless hookup, with
no strings attached and no complications afterward, might be just
what Lauren needed, although she'd never gone that far before.
Then Nalini's face flashed before her eyes, and she took a deep
breath.

"Enjoy the books." Lauren turned and walked away. She occupied herself with a few other tasks, straightening shelves that
didn't need to be straightened and rearranging books on the display tables, until the woman checked out.

Somehow, Lauren survived the rest of her shift without checking her phone every five minutes. When she got home, she was
surprised to see her mother's car in the driveway.

"I thought you were working tonight." Lauren tossed her purse
onto the coffee table.

"I was." Her mother followed Lauren into the kitchen. "Change
of plans. Apparently, Dave made a few adjustments to the schedule last night and neglected to tell me."

Lauren's mother had been the assistant manager at Hudson's,
the locally owned grocery store in Zachary, for almost a decade
now. She'd worked there for as long as Lauren could remember.
When the store manager retired three years earlier, her mother
had been really upset about not getting a promotion but, honestly,
Lauren didn't think her mother could have handled the job then.
The wounds from her brother Luke's death had been too fresh.
Even now, just thinking about him still choked Lauren up.

"Anyway," her mother continued, "since I'm home for dinner, how about Chinese takeout?"

Lauren took a long swig from the bottle of water she'd just retrieved from the fridge. "Works for me." She walked into her room and closed the door.

She checked her phone and thought about calling Josh to see if he wanted to join them for dinner, but she knew he'd probably be working. Weekends were usually busy at the garage, and Josh typically had Monday off. Maybe she'd catch up with him then, after spending her Sunday with Nalini—she hoped.

Lauren picked up the book she'd been reading and opened it to a bookmark, one she'd helped design for Great Expectations. She'd been looking forward to some quiet reading alone at home, and the change in her mother's schedule had thrown her off kilter more than she'd realized. Their relationship had improved considerably over the past year, after her mother had finally been able to quit drinking, but Lauren was used to eating dinner alone on most nights. As much as she hated to admit it, she was a creature of habit in many ways.

It wasn't until her mother returned with dinner a half-hour later, and the delicious aroma of soy sauce and stir-fried vegetables permeated the house, that Lauren realized how hungry she was. Her lunch had consisted of coffee and a complimentary, day-old blueberry muffin from Fleischmann's. Karl and Else Fleischmann treated Lauren as if she were their own daughter, and it was a rare occasion when she could leave their store without a carb-loaded but delicious baked treat—always on the house.

While her mother opened the takeout containers, Lauren grabbed a couple of plates and a roll of paper towels that served as napkins. She piled her plate with the house special mei fun and a generous portion of kung pao chicken, foregoing the white rice that accompanied the meals.

Her mother sat down across the table from Lauren. "So, how was your day?"

Lauren slurped the last bit of a noodle into her mouth and shrugged. "Busy. The last weekend before classes always is."

Fortunately, after confirming that Lauren had Sunday off, and reminding Lauren that she'd be working all day at Hudson's, her mother lapsed into silence again, for which Lauren was grateful. It wasn't like they didn't have anything to talk about, but ever since Luke's death, it seemed they were both more comfortable with keeping conversation to a minimum at the dinner table. Luke had always been the extrovert in the family, and sometimes Lauren wondered if he would have fallen in with the group of friends that he did, if he'd been more like her. She had never made friends easily all through school and her interrupted college years. It took a lot for her to trust someone enough to open up to them. Judging by what had happened with Kelly, trusting someone simply meant they would let you down sooner or later.

After dinner, Lauren did the dishes, and her mother settled down on the couch to watch TV. Lauren returned to her room and soon managed to immerse herself in her novel. A few times, though, she thought about texting to see how Nalini was doing. It took a fair amount of restraint for her to put down the phone again without unlocking it.

She ended up finishing her book just after midnight and finally sank into a restless sleep.

Her mother had already left for work by the time Lauren got out of bed Sunday morning. She grabbed a mug of coffee and settled on some toaster waffles for breakfast, liberally doused with maple syrup. The real kind, from the Carroll farm just off Route 1, east of Zachary. By the time she finished breakfast, her phone was still disappointingly silent.

Around nine, the phone pinged, and Lauren nearly dropped it after digging it out of the pocket of her jeans. She sighed. It was her mother.

Schedule change again. Will be home late tonight.

Lauren acknowledged the message. Weekends tended to make her mother's schedule even more unpredictable. She flipped through a few shows, then remembered the original plan for her day off. Catching up with *Quantico* would take her mind off Nalini...or make things worse. She sighed as she navigated to the first episode, when her phone pinged again. She grabbed it, her heart pounding.

This is Nalini. We met at the bookstore.

It was a good thing Nalini couldn't hear Lauren's heartbeat. *Yes, I remember.*

If you're free, I'd love to take you up on your offer and see the town.

Lauren took several long, deep breaths. Her first instinct was to respond with a string of emojis. Telling herself to act her age, she typed: *Sure! Want me to pick you up on campus?*

It's a beautiful day, and I can probably walk over. You live downtown, right? What's your address?

Lauren gave her directions and switched off the TV. She didn't want Nalini to show up and catch her drooling over PC. Why, Nalini might think she had an unhealthy obsession, or something...

After checking her hair in the mirror several times, Lauren sank into the comfort of the couch with another book. This time, she picked one of the classics: *Martin Chuzzlewit*, one of the few Dickens novels she hadn't read yet.

When the doorbell rang, she dropped the book in her haste. Her latent neat freak emerged, commanding her to pick it up and lay it on the coffee table. She ignored the urge and rushed to the door instead.

Nalini's lustrous hair was tied back in a ponytail. Considering that she'd just walked a mile, she looked perfect, and her full lips curved into an unconscious smile. Fighting an impulse to give Nalini a hug, Lauren ushered her into the living room.

"It really is a beautiful day," Lauren said. And it was—already in the mid-sixties, with only a few feathery clouds painted across the sky. The heat wave that Zachary had experienced for the past few days was beginning to fade, but the forecast called for temperatures in the upper seventies, which Lauren considered perfect for the season. "I thought we should spend as much of it outdoors as we can."

"That sounds great," Nalini said, glancing around the room. "I love your house, Lauren. I've always liked older houses, especially Cape Cods. This is a great neighborhood, too. You have a nice view of the river, and it's just a couple of blocks from the bookstore."

Lauren finally retrieved the book she'd dropped and returned it to a shelf. "Yeah, it's a great location." She grinned. "It makes living with your mother worthwhile."

"I'm not looking forward to winter, though. I've heard how brutal it can be up here."

"At least you were conditioned in Boston. If you had arrived here straight from India...well, I wouldn't want to be you."

Nalini laughed, tilting her head back and exposing her long, slender neck. Lauren longed to plant a kiss in the hollow at the base of Nalini's throat.

After Nalini declined an offer of something to drink, they decided to head out. Lauren led Nalini into the garage, and she eased into the seat beside Lauren. For a moment, Lauren wondered what Nalini thought of her ancient but trusty Outback wagon. She was glad she'd cleaned it out a few days earlier.

As Lauren started the car, she stole a quick glance at the delectable, smooth skin of Nalini's thighs while Nalini was busy fastening her seatbelt. Then Nalini turned to face Lauren, a smile lighting up her eyes.

"So, where are we going?"

"I figured we'd start at one of my favorite spots, Agate Beach. It's a pretty quiet beach in Powell Cove, just about twenty minutes south of Zachary. We may run into a few tourists, but most of them tend to go for the beach towns further south at this time of the year."

"Sounds perfect." Nalini's smile grew broader, and Lauren's heart jolted. She bit her lip, backed out of the driveway, and they were on their way.

SIX

NALINI EASED BACK into her seat as they sped down the two-lane road. Lauren had the windows partly down, and the breeze toyed with Nalini's hair despite her ponytail, blowing a few strands across her face. She swept them aside with one hand.

"Sorry," Lauren said. "I can roll the windows up, if you like."

"No, don't. This is perfect. I wish the weather was like this all year round."

Lauren chuckled. "Wait till you have your first Downeast winter. You'll appreciate this weather even more. How did you handle your first snowstorm in Boston?"

Nalini grinned. "Well, since I'd never really experienced snow before, I loved it. I wasn't driving, of course, otherwise I'd probably be cursing the roads like everyone else. The cold bothered me initially, but I got used to it."

"It's a little different up here." Lauren glanced out her window. "Kind of like Boston in some ways, but winter just seems longer. You can feel the cold all the way into your bones. I'm sure you'll adjust, though."

"Well, at least the accent is somewhat similar. I've been training myself to say *Bah Hah-bah* like a native Downeaster."

Lauren laughed. "Not bad. You'll fit right in."

The radio had been playing a selection of classic rock tunes, much to Nalini's delight. She'd have to find out what else she had in common with Lauren. The thought of exploring other things with Lauren brought a pleasant warmth to her cheeks, and she had to stop her imagination from running wild. As far as Nalini knew, Lauren was straight. Or was she? When they'd met, Nalini thought she'd picked up some signs of interest from Lauren, but that was before they'd talked about Josh.

When Boston's "More Than A Feeling" came on, Nalini reached for the control knob and turned up the volume. She rapped her fingers on the dashboard in time to the beat.

Lauren glanced at her before refocusing on the road. "You like Boston? The band, I mean. I would have thought it was a bit before your time."

"I like this song. Honestly, I can't remember most of their other songs, but this one has all sorts of memories for me. When I left home, a friend created a playlist on my phone with a bunch of music we used to listen to, as a parting gift. This was the first song on it." She smacked Lauren's thigh playfully. "And wouldn't it be before your time, too?"

With a chuckle, Lauren nodded. "I'm something of a classic rock junkie, I guess. You?"

Nalini shrugged. "I have fairly diverse tastes. I mean, anyone looking at my iPhone playlists would think I was really weird. I have stuff like Anoushka Shankar and Beethoven alongside Katy Perry and Lana Del Rey. It makes for some interesting combinations in shuffle mode."

"You know, I'd love to listen to that playlist from your friend the next time we get together. I'm afraid this old car radio doesn't have a Bluetooth connection."

Nalini turned her head in time to see the color rise in Lauren's cheeks.

"I mean...I wasn't assuming...that is, if we see each other again..."

Nalini's hand brushed across Lauren's thigh. She let it linger for just a few moments before pulling it away. "I know what you mean. I'd definitely like to hang out again some time. You're the only local I know here. And I really appreciate your taking the time to show me around like this."

"It's no big deal, really."

They rode in silence for a while, and Lauren left the volume on the radio turned up. Nalini stole another glance at Lauren's profile without trying to be too obvious. Lauren was a stunningly beautiful woman but, unlike her other relationships, Nalini was unsure of what, if anything, she should do. After all the arguments with her parents about arranged marriages, she'd decided it was best to keep things casual, no matter how attracted she might be to another woman. And she certainly didn't need to become a victim of "straight girl syndrome," like one of her friends at Wellesley had. For now, it was best for them to remain friends.

When a commercial came on, Lauren turned down the volume. The road narrowed, and Nalini spotted a sign for Agate Beach.

"This part of town was all there was to Zachary when it was founded," Lauren said, taking a left. "It was really more of a fishing village than anything else, like many of the coastal towns, but it grew quickly into a seaport. It's hard to imagine the town celebrated its two hundred fiftieth anniversary a few years ago."

Nalini took several deep breaths as the unmistakable scent of the ocean grew stronger. Most of the houses they passed had boats in their driveways or yards. As they rounded a curve in the road, Nalini caught her first glimpse of the sparkling blue waters of the bay. They passed a corner grocery store and a bar, and Nalini smiled.

"You know, I always used to take issue with tourist brochures that described towns as 'quaint,' but it fits perfectly in this case."

"I agree." Lauren flashed a smile that made Nalini's pulse quicken. "I love coming out here to the old section of town. It's like going back in time."

Lauren pulled off the main road, taking a winding path with dense stands of evergreen trees lining either side. Nalini barely managed to make out the sign, nearly hidden by low branches, that read Powell Cove State Park in faded letters. There was only one other car in the small parking lot when they arrived.

They got out of the car and headed along a trail covered with rust-brown wood chips. Nalini inhaled slowly, savoring the salt in the air. The trees began to thin out after a while, and she could her the faint hiss and roar of the surf.

"Welcome to Agate Beach," Lauren said, spreading her arms wide.

Gravel crunched under Nalini's feet, and she gasped as the view opened up before her. A broad stretch of multicolored gravel and pebbles extended before her to the surf line. At the water's edge, a few spotted sandpipers scurried back and forth, following the path of the waves as they washed up and broke over the shore.

"There isn't really a lot of agate left," Lauren said, turning to look at Nalini. "The cliffs up there," she waved a hand, "are mostly amygdaloidal basalt, so there's many different varieties of rocks that make up the beach. I guess they were all carried along here when the lava flowed out to the ocean and cooled." She slapped a hand to her forehead. "Look at me—talking about lava flows to a scientist."

"Well, I'm really a biologist by training, although I did take a geology class for one semester." Nalini shaded her eyes with one hand, scanning the ocean. "You know way more about the area than I do. This would be an awesome place to do some field research, though. I bet there's all kinds of microbial life here that I know very little about."

They walked forward until the tide lapped at their feet. Nalini bent down and waited for the next gentle wave, letting it caress her fingers. "I can see why you like this place, Lauren. It's beautiful." She wanted to add, "just like you," but apart from it being a tired cliché, Nalini had promised herself to keep the conversation from drifting into dangerous territory.

And yet, she got the sense that Lauren's eyes were boring into her back. She turned around, but Lauren's sunglasses made it difficult for Nalini to read her expression. Was she just imagining things? Nalini crouched lower and picked up a handful of pebbles. "Maybe I'll get lucky and find some agate." She almost bit her tongue as she realized that Lauren might interpret the first part of her sentence in an entirely different way.

"Let's see what you've got." Lauren's hands cupped hers, and Nalini swallowed. "Hmm...most of the reddish-brown ones are rhyolite, from what I remember. Of course, there's plenty of quartz. People still come out here hunting for agates, though."

Nalini tried to slow down her breathing. She hoped Lauren hadn't noticed her reaction.

"I don't think there's any agate." Lauren pulled her hands away, and Nalini couldn't help feeling a twinge of disappointment. "It can be hard to recognize, though, except for the banded variety. Those are really shiny and pretty distinctive. Keep looking."

The gentle rhythm of the waves lulled Nalini into a trance-like state that was broken only by the occasional, piercing cries of the seagulls circling overhead. Every once in a while, she stopped to scoop up some more pebbles. After examining them, she'd offer them to Lauren, who would shake her head. They walked further along the shoreline in the direction of a lighthouse that stood on a rocky promontory, like a thick finger pointing into the bay. Lauren joined in Nalini's treasure hunt, occasionally squatting and picking up a few pebbles of her own.

They had almost reached the base of the promontory when Lauren stopped and called out to Nalini, who was lagging behind, watching a pair of sandpipers chase the surf.

"I think I've got one." Lauren straightened up, smiling.

Nalini caught up to her and peered at the stone in Lauren's hand. It was perfectly smooth, about the size of a robin's egg, with a striated pattern in varying shades of gray and tan.

"It's a banded agate." Lauren cupped Nalini's hands in hers, once again making Nalini's pulse speed up. She pressed the stone into Nalini's hand. "You keep it. I have plenty at home. A little souvenir of your first visit to Agate Beach."

The simple gesture touched Nalini more than she wanted to admit at that moment, leaving her at a loss for words. She gave Lauren's hand a quick squeeze and slipped the agate into a pocket.

Soon, they turned around and headed back along the shore. Nalini lost track of time as she savored the untamed beauty of their surroundings. The few shorebirds running away from them as they walked, or circling overhead, were their only companions. She glanced at Lauren again, admiring her flawless complexion, delicate cheekbones, and full, pink lips. She wondered how Lauren's lips would taste...

Nalini shook her head and took a step forward. Her foot hit something hard, slipped out from under her and, with a yelp, she tumbled down onto the coarse sand.

"Are you okay?" Lauren was by her side in a second, extending her hand. "You must have tripped on that piece of driftwood."

Nalini nodded, trying to hide her embarrassment. "I'm fine." Still, she let Lauren pull her upright. For a moment, they were close enough that she could spot a stray eyelash that had fallen onto Lauren's cheek. Her heart beat faster as Lauren's lips parted.

Then Lauren released her hand, breaking the spell.

SEVEN

LAUREN WOULD GLADLY have spent all day walking along the beach with Nalini. Every instinct was telling her this was a stupid mistake, driven by her hopeless infatuation with Priyanka Chopra. Nalini had caught Lauren's eye from the first moment when she'd walked into the bookstore. As they walked further, Lauren was forced to admit that her obsession with the Bollywood star and model wasn't the only reason she was drawn to Nalini.

She really liked Nalini. Although she certainly found Nalini physically attractive, Lauren genuinely enjoyed just being with her. There were a few people whose company Lauren enjoyed, like Jen and Josh, but this was different. More than once, she'd had to restrain herself from reaching out to take Nalini's hand. It felt like the most natural gesture in the world. That one time, when Lauren had helped Nalini get up after she'd tripped, had been almost more than Lauren could bear. The sensation of Nalini's soft, warm hand in hers...Lauren had done everything in her power to stop herself from pulling Nalini even closer and kissing her.

As the sun climbed high overhead, Lauren realized they hadn't made lunch plans as yet. She checked the time on her phone.

"Would you like to get some lunch? There's a couple of great seafood restaurants in this part of town, or we could go back to the downtown area."

"Lunch sounds lovely," Nalini said. "There's just one issue, though. I'm a vegetarian, so I'm afraid seafood is out."

Lauren ran through the list of options in her mind. "We should head back, then. There's a great pizza place in town—Romano's. I'm pretty sure they have at least one vegetarian option. I've never tried it, but I usually just get the same thing every time."

Nalini threw back her head and laughed.

"Um...is that a no to pizza?"

"I'm sorry. Pizza would be fine. It just reminded me of yesterday, when I met this guy, Paul, at my dorm. He gave me one of his frozen pizzas. It was so sweet of him. We went out for drinks last night, too."

Lauren's heart sank down into her shoes, her visions of stealing that first kiss evaporating like the morning fog that often filled the cove. She took a deep breath. "Well, I'm sure Romano's will be much better. It's just down the street from the bookstore. After lunch, we can take a walk around downtown, not that there's a lot to see. That is, if you have the time."

"You're really spoiling me, you know." Nalini squeezed Lauren's arm, sending a warming shiver through her. "Although, as an only child, I should warn you I'm used to it."

They walked back to the car, Lauren now more confused than ever. She was on the verge of confessing to Nalini that her interest went beyond friendship, but something held her back. Instead, she steered the conversation to a safer topic.

"How long have you been a vegetarian?"

"All my life, really."

"So, it's a religious thing?" Lauren had heard that a lot of Indians were vegetarians, but her knowledge of the country didn't extend much beyond the worlds of the few Indian authors whose books she'd read.

"Well, I guess it started out that way. I'm not particularly religious, much to my parents' disappointment. I just don't think raising and killing animals for food on a massive scale is necessary or environmentally sound."

Lauren frowned. "But won't you be working on animals? In your research, I mean?"

"You have a point. I know it sounds weird, a marine biologist not wanting to eat animals. Actually, my research will focus on saltwater microbial species. I'll probably be spending more time staring at stuff through a microscope than dissecting anything."

"Sorry if I'm being nosy. I do understand, especially about the whole factory farming thing. I'd thought about going vegan a few times when I was at Orono, because I knew a girl who was. But I could never bring myself to do it. I guess I like the taste of dead animals too much."

"I'm sure I could convert you." Nalini giggled, and Lauren laughed along with her.

The feeling's mutual, Lauren thought, though perhaps not quite in the way Nalini was thinking.

When they walked into Romano's, the yeasty odor of fresh-baked dough made Lauren's mouth water. She handed a menu to Nalini and walked up to the counter.

"Hey, Lauren! I was wondering if I'd see you today." The man behind the counter winked at Lauren. "The usual for you?"

Lauren nodded. "Of course. Tony, this is my friend, Nalini. She's a new grad student at the university. Nalini, Tony owns this place."

Nalini put down the menu and giggled as Tony performed an exaggerated bow. "Your name's really Tony Romano?"

"What can I say? It's a curse." He spread his hands and laughed.

"Tony's the real deal," Lauren said, "or as close as you can get. Third-generation Italian family. You won't find better pizza up or down the coast."

"Flattery doesn't work on me, you know." Tony turned to Lauren. "Despite those beautiful blue eyes and gorgeous smile, you still have to pay for your meal. Your friend, though...we'll see about her. What'll you have, sweetheart?"

"A personal-size veggie deluxe, please." Nalini batted her eyelashes, making Lauren giggle. "And a diet Coke."

"Coming right up." Tony punched a few keys at the cash register. "I'll bring them to your table. And, because this is your friend's first visit to my humble establishment, how about a couple of garden salads on the house?"

Lauren accepted with enthusiasm and handed over her credit card, just as Nalini reached into her purse. "My treat. You're new here, remember? Besides, I feel compelled to help out poor, starving grad students."

Nalini's eyes sparkled. "Starving, maybe, but that's as far as it goes. Well, I'll make sure I get the next one, then."

Their eyes locked for a moment, and then they both burst out laughing. Lauren collected their sodas, and they made their way to a corner table near the window.

Their salads arrived soon after they sat down, carried across by a girl whom Lauren hadn't seen before. With summer help vanishing, it was the time of year for many of the Main Street merchants to make new hires. Nalini laughed as Tony winked at Lauren again before disappearing into the kitchen.

"Does he flirt with all his customers like that?"

Lauren grinned. "Pretty much. Well, with the women, anyway. He took a special interest in me, though, for some reason, and he enjoyed flirting with me when we met. Now, I think he does it just because it's become a habit."

Nalini slurped her soda, her gaze never leaving Lauren's. "Not quite your type?"

"Well, apart from the fact that he's almost old enough to be my father, no. Actually, I prefer..." Lauren clapped a hand over her mouth.

"You prefer younger guys? That's entirely understandable." Nalini's expression was unreadable.

Something clicked inside Lauren's head, and she leaned forward. Even though it had been less than a day they'd spent together, she really wanted Nalini as a friend. Based on the little she knew about Nalini's conservative family background, what she was about to reveal could very well spell the end of their brief friendship.

"Actually, Nalini, I'm a lesbian." There. It was done.

"Oh, thank god!" Nalini reached for Lauren's hand and squeezed it. Not exactly the reaction Lauren had expected, but it sent a thrill running through her entire body, nevertheless.

"This is...this makes you happy?"

"Of course. You see, I'm one too, although my family doesn't know. I've been waiting for the right time to tell you, but I wasn't sure how you might react." Nalini stabbed at a cherry tomato with her fork. "I'm so glad you told me."

Lauren leaned back in her chair and exhaled slowly. A wave of relief washed over her, which soon gave way to a new sense of excitement. "So...are you in a relationship? If not, is this a date?"

Nalini looked at Lauren from under her long, thick eyelashes. "Do you want it to be?"

"Well, I'm not seeing anyone." Lauren tried to keep the disappointment out of her voice, but a note of it crept into the overly dramatic sigh that followed. "Are you?"

"No. I guess it's a date, then. I'm glad."

The warmth in Nalini's eyes made Lauren's heart thump erratically.

Their pizzas arrived, brought to the table not by the waitress who'd stirred Lauren's interest earlier, but by Tony himself. After reassuring him several times that there was nothing else they needed, Nalini pushed aside the remnants of her salad. "I take it Tony doesn't know?"

"No. Very few people here do. It's a small town and, apart from campus, it's more conservative than you might expect."

Just as Lauren reached for her pizza, her phone rang. She glanced at the display, which showed a call from Hudson's. That was weird. Her mother never used the store phone.

"Sorry, I have to get this," she said, pushing her chair back. She walked to the door and stepped outside. "This is Lauren."

"Lauren, this is Dave from Hudson's. I'm sorry to disturb you, but it's your mother. She had an accident at the store."

EIGHT

NALINI LOOKED UP as Lauren returned to the table. All the color had drained from Lauren's cheeks, and her hand shook as she rested it on the chair.

"What's wrong?" Nalini longed to put her arms around Lauren, even if she didn't quite know what was going on.

"It's my mother. She's in the hospital. Something about passing out and falling at work. I'm really sorry, but I have to go. They think she'll be okay, but I've got to see her."

"I'll come with you." Nalini grabbed the cardboard boxes in which their pizzas were served and closed the lids, leaving the remnants of their salads on the table.

"Are you sure? I can drop you off near campus, if you like. It's on the way. Bayview's not far, just about ten minutes from here."

"Don't be silly. You look like you could use a friend right now."

Lauren's cornflower blue eyes glistened, and she put an arm around Nalini's shoulder. "Thank you," she whispered.

"Do you know what happened?" Nalini rolled down her window a crack as Lauren pulled out of the municipal parking lot behind Romano's and turned onto Main Street.

"I'm not sure. The assistant manager, Dave—he's the one who called—said she hit her head on some shelving. I don't know how all the details, though. They called 911 right away."

Nalini let Lauren drive in silence the rest of the way, sensing that she needed the time to process what had happened. The aroma of their pizzas wafted across from the back seat, but Nalini's appetite had been blunted, and she barely noticed. Her mind drifted back to their long walk on the beach. All that time, she'd been wondering why she was so attracted to Lauren, and telling herself it was useless to even hope that something might develop between them. If she'd only acted on her impulse...

She shook her head and gazed out the window. There wasn't much traffic on Route 1 as they passed the junction with Route 1A and headed south. They reached Bayview Hospital in under the ten minutes that Lauren had predicted.

A quick inquiry at the desk led them to a room on the third floor. The door was ajar, and Lauren rapped on it with her knuckles before charging in. Nalini stood in the doorway, suddenly unsure of herself.

An older version of Lauren looked up at them. Nalini was struck by the resemblance. Lauren's mother had the same mesmerizing blue eyes and sandy blonde hair, although some of it was hidden by a bandage that wrapped around her head.

Lauren ran to the bedside and threw her arms around her mother. "I was so worried. Are you okay?"

Lauren's mother extricated herself from the bear hug. "The doctor thinks I'll be fine, apart from a nasty gash on the back of my head." She touched her bandage with one finger and winced. "They want to keep me here overnight, but he said I'd be able to go home tomorrow if the test results are okay. I'll have to take a few days off work, though."

"How did it happen?"

"I don't really know. One minute I was helping Dave with inventory, and the next I was on the floor. Apparently, I had a sudden drop in blood pressure. There could be a number of causes, the doctor said, so they're running some tests and have called in an endocrinologist. The doctor thinks it could be related to thyroid function. I have a mild concussion from hitting my head, which is why I have to stay overnight. They'll do another evaluation tomorrow."

For the first time, Lauren's mother noticed Nalini, who was still hovering in the doorway, and gave her a weak smile.

Lauren turned her head, following her mother's gaze. "Oh god...I'm sorry. I'm not thinking straight. Mom, this is Nalini. She's a friend from the university."

Nalini stepped forward. "I'm so glad you're going to be okay, Mrs. Clarke."

"Thank you, Nalini. And please call me Michelle."

They spent an hour in the hospital room, and Nalini was pleased to see Lauren's spirits lighten as time went by, until she was almost back to her old self.

Secretly, Nalini craved the kind of relationship that Lauren appeared to have with her mother. Despite the age difference, the two of them seemed more like sisters than mother and daughter. Most of all, Michelle's easy acceptance of Nalini's presence, without asking a single question about how they'd met or why she'd chosen to accompany Lauren, set Nalini at ease—something her own mother could rarely do. Nalini had always got along better with her father, but he wasn't home much. When he was, their conversations were mostly about her classes, or Bollywood movies. Nalini didn't particularly care for them, mostly watching English moves instead.

They left after Lauren promised her mother she'd be back first thing in the morning. She reached for Nalini's hand as they headed for the elevator. "I really appreciate the company."

Nalini's hand lingered in Lauren's briefly, their fingers intertwined until the elevator arrived, and they stepped inside. Lauren pressed the button for the underground parking garage.

They walked toward Lauren's Outback. As soon as she opened the door, the smell of pizza sauce and melted cheese overwhelmed Nalini, and her stomach growled in response.

"No wonder I'm starving," Lauren said, checking the time. "Well, we still have food. Would you like to come over? I can reheat the pizzas in the oven for a few minutes."

"That would be great." Nalini eased into her seat. "I like your mom. I really hope this all turns out okay. You two seem to have a pretty close relationship."

Lauren glanced at Nalini before backing out of her spot. "It wasn't always like this." They approached the exit. Lauren gave the attendant her validated parking ticket, and the metal bar swung up to let them through.

"Was it difficult...coming out to her?" Nalini suspected the reaction from her parents, if she ever had the courage to broach the subject, would be quite different.

"Not really. Actually, it was easier than I thought. It's just that I'd been putting it off, and there was never really a good time. I was more concerned about what my brother would think, in some ways."

"I didn't know you have a brother. So, he doesn't like his sister being gay? Does he think you're going to steal his girlfriends, or something?"

For a moment, Lauren didn't answer. She continued looking straight ahead at the road, and Nalini had to strain her ears to catch Lauren's response.

"I had a brother. He died a few years ago."

At that moment, Nalini felt small enough to crawl under the floor mat. "God, Lauren, I'm sorry. Me and my big mouth."

"It's okay. Luke was fine with me coming out. Actually, I think he would have liked you. He could be pretty charming. When he was sober, that is."

Nalini opened her mouth but decided not to venture further on already thin ice and shut it again.

"It was what killed him." Lauren's hands tightened on the wheel. Once again, Nalini longed to take Lauren in her arms and hold her tight. "Booze and drugs. He slammed his car into a utility pole on Route 1 near Jonesboro."

Lauren's voice had a hard edge to it that made Nalini glad she hadn't asked any questions. All things considered, it was best just to let Lauren talk, if she needed to.

"After the accident, mom was a wreck. It wasn't enough that she enabled my brother's drinking, but she was hitting the bottle pretty hard herself. I dropped out of college to move back here and take care of her. I guess I didn't want to see her end up the same way as Luke." Lauren bit her lower lip. "We barely spoke to each other for the first week after the funeral."

All of Nalini's tumultuous relationship with her parents seemed to pale into insignificance as she listened to Lauren. "I'm sorry." It sounded so inadequate, but it was all Nalini could say. She couldn't imagine what losing her brother would feel like. The urge to comfort Lauren, and ease the pain that was so evident in her voice, grew even stronger.

When they got out of the car, Nalini gave in at last. She pulled Lauren into her arms and held her for a while, stroking her hair. Lauren's body relaxed against hers, and Nalini could sense some of the tension draining.

"Thank you," Lauren said, blinking away tears. "I really needed that."

They went inside and finished their late lunch. Nalini stretched her legs, sinking into the comfortable couch. She brushed aside her anxiety about starting her first semester at a new college, something that had haunted her the night before. All of those issues didn't seem nearly as important as they did just twenty-four hours ago. For now, being with Lauren just felt right.

"I guess the tour of the town will have to wait," Lauren said. She leaned forward, and Nalini felt herself drowning in the depths of those sparkling blue eyes. Her breathing sped up.

"That's okay. We have plenty of time." Nalini could hear herself speaking, but her voice seemed to come from somewhere far away. It had been a long time since a woman had affected her like this. Her mind wandered back to her last relationship for a moment. She knew she could never let it get to the serious stage, and they'd parted on good terms during their senior year. It still hurt on occasion, though, and Nalini had already made up her mind not to get involved again. And yet, when Lauren looked at her like that...

"Nalini?" Lauren snapped her fingers. "You still here?"

"Um...sorry. I guess my mind wandered for a bit. What were you saying?"

"I was wondering if you wouldn't mind staying here with me tonight."

NINE

LAUREN REALIZED HOW her request must sound, and heat blossomed in her cheeks. "I didn't mean it like that. I just don't want to be alone tonight. If you don't have any plans, that is...I'd really appreciate it."

"Of course." The warmth in Nalini's eyes made Lauren melt. "I'd be happy to."

"I think we're about the same size, so you can borrow some of my clothes if you need to. This means a lot. Thank you." Lauren flung her arms around Nalini and hugged her. As her breasts pressed against Nalini's, Lauren became acutely aware of a stirring deep within her—one she hadn't experienced for a long time. She let go of Nalini, but the delicate sandalwood scent of Nalini's perfume lingered, and it took every ounce of Lauren's self-control to stop her from reaching for Nalini again.

For a moment, Lauren regretted her invitation to Nalini. Her mother was going to be fine. It seemed silly to be so upset over what was, in all likelihood, just a minor medical condition. And yet, Lauren had instinctively imagined the worst when she'd got the phone call, triggering memories of the one she'd received several years ago about Luke. She did her best to shrug the feeling off.

They spent the evening eating leftovers in front of the TV. Lauren grabbed a couple of sodas and settled back on the couch next to Nalini. She was reaching for the remote when her phone buzzed.

Heard about your mom. Hope she's okay. Are you home?

It would be just like Josh to hear the news. He seemed to know everything that was going on in Zachary, and Lauren had long since given up trying to figure out how.

She tapped the message to reply. *Yes. Want to come over?*

Be there in ten.

Noticing Nalini's raised eyebrow, Lauren grinned. "Sorry. It's just Josh. You don't mind if he comes over, do you?"

"Not at all." Nalini smiled. "I have to admit when you first told me about him, I was...well, I thought you two were in a relationship."

Lauren threw her head back and laughed. "Me and Josh? That's a good one."

When Josh arrived, he flung his arms around Lauren as soon as she opened the door, and then froze in the middle of the hallway. "I'm sorry. I didn't realize you had company."

"It's okay, really. I was hoping you two would get a chance to meet." Lauren dragged him into the living room. "This is Nalini. She's new in town. She went with me to the hospital today."

"Nice to meet you." Josh shook Nalini's hand and then turned back to Lauren with the hint of a question in his eyes.

Lauren knew that look well. She refrained from saying anything, silently encouraging Josh to draw his own conclusions.

He sank into an armchair. "How's your mom?"

"They think she'll be okay. She has a cut on her head from falling, but I don't think there's anything seriously wrong. We'll find out more tomorrow, after they do some more tests, but she should be coming home." Seeing Josh's nod of acceptance once again made Lauren question her request to Nalini earlier. It really did seem silly to ask someone she'd barely known for a day to spend the night at her house. And yet, knowing that Nalini would be there had already eased much of Lauren's anxiety.

"So, how do you like Zachary so far?" Josh turned to Nalini, favoring her with a smile that lit up his eyes.

"It's been great so far. Lauren took me to Agate Beach this morning, and I loved it."

"Ah, so you've seen Lauren's favorite spot." Josh winked at Lauren, who fought the urge to throw something at him. "You're lucky. She doesn't share that with too many people." He turned to Lauren. "You should have come by the garage."

"Josh is a mechanic at Henry's Garage," Lauren told Nalini. "We passed it on the way to the beach earlier."

Nalini nodded. "Yes, I remember. Do you enjoy working with cars, Josh?"

He grinned. "I'm a musician, really. Being a mechanic pays the bills, though."

Lauren rolled her eyes. "Sorry, how could I forget? Yes, Josh plays in a band."

"What do you play?" Nalini leaned forward, her eyes sparkling.

"Guitar, mostly. It's just me and a few other guys. We do a lot of covers. I've written some songs, but our audience seems to like covers best. You should come check us out. We're playing in town Wednesday night."

"I'd love to," Nalini said.

"Great! Just promise not to throw anything at us." Josh's grin changed to a pensive expression, and he raised a hand to his head. "You know, you remind me of someone. I can't quite place it, but..."

Nalini shot a glance at Lauren, and then both of them burst out laughing.

"I should have known, seeing as how you're a friend of Lauren's." Nalini wiped her eyes with the back of her hand. "I don't watch a lot of TV, I'm afraid."

Seeing Josh's puzzled expression, Lauren decided to take pity on him. "What's my favorite TV show, Josh?"

His frown deepened, and then it was almost as if Lauren could see the light bulb coming on above his head.

"Oh my god. No wonder Lauren likes you."

Once again, Lauren was seized by an urge to throw something at Josh. This time, she yielded to the impulse, although it was only a cushion, and he caught it before it could do any damage.

Lauren left Josh and Nalini to chatter on while she grabbed another soda from the fridge. As Josh and Nalini discussed their favorite bands, Lauren stole glances at Nalini out of the corner of her eye. She really was beautiful. Her long, silky hair caught the fading sunlight that streamed in through the picture window, forming a glimmering aura around her face. Lauren's pulse hammered in her ears as she let her gaze travel along the curve of Nalini's neck, imagining her lips tasting that gorgeous brown skin.

It was over an hour later when Josh left, after extracting a promise from Lauren to call him if she needed help when her mother got home from the hospital.

"He's nice," Nalini said, tilting her head toward the door. "How long have you two known each other?"

Lauren grinned. "Since I was in kindergarten."

Nalini pursed her lips. "Did he and you ever...I mean, before you knew..."

"Josh and me? Oh god, no! Nothing like that. Actually, he was the first person I told when I figured out I was a lesbian. I was thirteen at the time, and he's a year older. He's been like a brother, really."

Nalini lowered her gaze. "I sometimes wish I had a brother I could confide in. It would probably make things easier with my parents, because they wouldn't be so focused on me. Although there are certainly benefits to being an only child."

As evening faded and dissolved into night, Lauren found herself imagining what it would be like to have Nalini there with her every night. They came from such different backgrounds, and Lauren was more than a little envious about Nalini's apparent lack of concern with financial matters. Yet, in the ways that mattered, the two of them being together felt so right.

When Nalini stifled a yawn, Lauren jumped up from the couch. "I'm sorry. You probably have an early day tomorrow. Are you taking a full class load?"

"More or less. First-year graduate students generally try to get all their coursework requirements out of the way in the first two or three semesters, so they can focus on research later." Nalini stood up and stretched, and Lauren carefully averted her eyes after a tantalizing glimpse of Nalini's breasts straining against her T shirt. "What I'm really dreading, though, is being a teaching assistant. I know what a brat I was as a freshman at Wellesley. I can't imagine teaching kids just like me!"

Lauren walked down the hallway and rummaged in the linen closet. "I'm sure you'll do fine. By the way, you can use the bed in the guest room. Just give me a few minutes to change the sheets."

"Are you sure? The couch would be fine, you know."

"Of course I'm sure. You need to get a good night's sleep before your first day of classes. It'll be way more comfortable than the couch."

A short while later, Nalini had gratefully accepted an oversized sleep shirt and a new toothbrush from Lauren. She emerged from the bathroom, and Lauren's chest tightened with a flash of desire. Nalini looked so good in that shirt. Lauren vowed not to wash it so she could sleep with it on her pillow and inhale Nalini's delicious, sandalwood scent...

What was wrong with her? She'd never been this giddy, even when she'd started dating Kelly.

By the time she'd made sure Nalini was comfortable, and she'd settled into her own bed, Lauren was wide awake. It took an hour of tossing and turning, trying to find a comfortable position, before she flopped down on her stomach with one arm dangling off the bed and finally sank into oblivion.

The dreams that had haunted her for the past few years returned. She gripped the edge of the seat as the car hurtled down the highway, the torrential rain drumming on the hood. The wipers squeaked and cut brief patches of clarity through which Lauren could glimpse the blanket of water covering the road.

"Slow down, Luke." Her heart hammered against her ribs. "You're going to get us killed."

She blinked as the twin beams of an oncoming vehicle lit up the windshield. The car swerved, and Luke cursed. Then Lauren saw the tall outline of the utility pole rushing toward them, and her eyes widened.

"Oh my god, we're going to—"

She screamed. Then there was nothing but inky blackness.

"Lauren? Are you okay?"

Warm arms cradled Lauren's head. Lauren's chest heaved with the effort to breathe, and a soft whimper escaped from her throat. She leaned back against the delicious softness of Nalini's breasts.

"Was it a bad dream? I was up getting some water, and I heard you scream." Nalini's fingers trailed down Lauren's neck.

Lauren nodded. It took a few moments before she could speak. "I have the same dream every once in a while. I'm in the car with Luke just before he crashes, even though I wasn't there when it happened. Maybe it's because I feel like if I only had been there with him that night, it wouldn't have happened."

"You can't blame yourself." Nalini's arms tightened around Lauren. "It's not your fault."

"I know. I've tried to convince myself of that for a while. And yet, there are times..." Lauren turned her head to see Nalini looking down at her, dark eyes shadowed in the diffuse moonlight that filtered through the window blinds.

Slowly, Nalini's head moved closer. Lauren's breath caught in her throat.

Nalini's lips brushed against hers, tentatively. Her hand grazed Lauren's cheek.

Lauren's lips parted, and then Nalini was kissing her with urgency, her tongue thrusting into Lauren's mouth. Lauren welcomed it, teasing it with her own.

They pulled apart at last, and Lauren sucked in great mouthfuls of air. Her heart felt like it was about to burst from her chest. She could still taste the sweetness of Nalini's lips. She sat up, one hand still in Nalini's lap.

"Nalini...I..."

"We can't do this, Lauren." Nalini sighed. "I want you so much, but I can't get involved with anyone right now. I don't want to hurt you."

Lauren's heart sank. "Shouldn't you let me be the judge of that?"

Nalini took Lauren's hand. "I'm sorry. I just...I wanted to comfort you, and I let myself get carried away. It would be just sex, but what I really need now is a friend. Can you do that?"

Thinking that "just sex" wouldn't be such a bad thing at the moment, Lauren nodded. "If that's what you want."

TEN

AS LUCK WOULD have it, Nalini's first class of the day was taught by the professor she hoped to select as her research advisor. The core biology class was required for all graduate students in the program. Despite her mind wandering, and a general fogginess caused by not getting enough sleep the night before, Nalini made a superhuman effort to appear attentive and interested, even asking a few questions at just the right times. The size of the class surprised her, compared to her higher-level undergraduate classes at Wellesley. There were only a dozen students scattered around the classroom.

Fortunately, the next class was more suited to Nalini's state of mind. The professor's monotone, combined with the subject matter, applied statistics for biologists, soon had Nalini spacing out and stifling a yawn. She wasn't the only one, apparently. A quick glance around the room revealed that most of her fellow first-year graduate students were in a similar state of torpor.

After returning to bed in the guest room the previous night, Nalini had spent the better part of an hour replaying the incident with Lauren over and over in her mind. For a while, she had to resist the overwhelming temptation to rush back into Lauren's bedroom for another kiss...and more.

She wanted Lauren. There was no getting around that. And, judging by Lauren's reaction to that kiss, the feeling was mutual. The energy that had sparked between them, the softness of Lauren's lips, the warmth of Lauren's breath, the delicious sensation of Lauren's stiff nipples rubbing against her for a brief moment...

Nalini's head jerked upright as the professor dismissed the class to an audible groan of relief from the students. She slung her backpack over her shoulder and checked her schedule. As she turned toward the door, a hand brushed against her arm.

"Hey, you're in the grad student dorms, right? I think I saw you there this weekend."

Nalini looked up to see a pair of brown eyes, flecked with gold, staring at her. Her companion had short, straight black hair with bangs that enhanced the beauty of her delicate features.

"I'm Emi." She held out a hand, and Nalini took it. "This is my first semester here."

"Nalini. And yes, you're right, I do live in Jorgensen." Nalini's gaze roamed over Emi's face, dwelling on her delicate, upturned nose and sumptuous lips. "I'm a new grad student, too. Are you in the marine biology program? I don't think you were at the department orientation this morning."

"No, I'm actually in the biochemistry division, but the graduate advisor told me to take this statistics course." Emi giggled. "I must say I'm beginning to doubt her wisdom already."

Nalini rolled her eyes. "I know, right?" She glanced over her shoulder, but the professor had already left the classroom. Still, she lowered her voice and leaned closer to Emi. "This is shaping up to be the dullest class I've ever taken."

They walked out the door together. "So, I'm guessing you're from India?" Emi turned to Nalini, her captivating eyes twinkling.

"You guessed right. I did my undergrad at Wellesley, so I've been in the US a little over four years now. How about you?"

"My parents are Japanese-American, but I was born in Lewiston. I've lived in Maine all my life." Emi checked her phone. "Well, I have to be off to my next class. It's analytical chemistry. I hope it's going to be better than this one. I'll see you around the dorms, right?"

"Absolutely. Enjoy the rest of your day." Nalini watched Emi as she walked away, enjoying the way her trim ass swayed gently.

What was wrong with her? Had she really sunk so low that she was checking out every woman she met? Her gaydar seemed to be on the fritz, too, which didn't help any. Then again, it had been almost a year since Nalini had been sexually involved with anyone. She hoped nobody could smell her desperation. A large part of it now was fueled by what had happened or, rather, not happened with Lauren the previous night.

She shook her head. She had a break before her next class, so she decided to head over to the science library, one area of the campus that she hadn't yet had an opportunity to check out.

Nalini didn't hear from Lauren until Wednesday afternoon. Fortunately, her classes and the adjustment to her new life on campus had kept her busy enough, so that she had little time to think about anything else.

She suppressed a smile when Lauren's message popped up on her laptop during a class.

Looking forward to tonight?

Trying to keep her attention on the professor at the front of the room, Nalini responded. *Yes, can't wait.*

Me too. I'll pick you up at Jorgensen around 7.

Nalini confirmed, realizing she was looking forward to seeing Lauren far more than an evening of live music at a bar. She wondered if Lauren felt the same way. Her mind drifted back to that kiss, and how it could have led to so much more if she hadn't pulled back. Not for the first time, she questioned whether she'd made the right decision.

After checking her phone a few minutes before seven o'clock, Nalini began pacing around her room. When her phone pinged finally, she grabbed a jacket and raced down the three flights of stairs, deciding not to wait for the elevator. By the time she slid into the car seat beside Lauren, she was breathing heavily.

Lauren raised an eyebrow. "Are you okay?"

"Just...catching my breath."

Lauren grinned. "I didn't realize I had such an effect on you."

If Lauren only knew. "Don't flatter yourself." Nalini smacked her on the arm.

Still grinning, Lauren eased the car away from the curb. "Well, you've made it halfway through your first week of classes. How's your teaching assignment been going?"

"Actually, I don't know yet. I've only had to sit in for one upper-level biology class that my research advisor...my prospective research advisor, rather...is teaching. The freshman labs don't start until next week, but I'm not really worried about those. I have to actually teach one class a week, which is basically just a review session, but the thought of standing up there in front of those kids..."

Lauren laughed as they headed away from campus toward Route 1. "Just don't try to picture them all naked. That never seemed to work for me in high school when I had to give a presentation before the class."

When they drove into town, Nalini couldn't keep her mind off an image that banished everything else from her mind—Lauren sitting in a classroom all by herself, completely naked.

Just then, Lauren glanced at Nalini, and the warmth in her eyes sent Nalini's pulse racing again. She did her best to tear her mind away from the tantalizing image of a naked Lauren stretched out in a classroom chair before they arrived.

It was the first time Nalini had been in a small-town bar, and she surveyed the room as they entered. The dim lighting and dark, wood-paneled walls intrigued her, giving the place more character than the few more upscale bars she'd visited in Boston. It definitely had a different vibe from the one Paul had taken her to on

Saturday night. She glanced at the solitary pool table at the back of the bar with interest. A few of her friends at Wellesley had introduced her to pool, but Nalini had soon realized she had little or no aptitude for the game. At the time, she'd blamed it on the bar's half-price cocktails.

Lauren directed Nalini's attention to a small area across from the bar that had been cleared of tables. The band was still tuning up, and Josh waved at them as they looked around the room. There were still a few empty tables, and Lauren guided Nalini to one near the back.

"What would you like to drink?"

Nalini thought for a moment. "I acquired a taste for Scotch, thanks to my uncle, but tonight I think I'll go with a Long Island. Actually, I wouldn't mind some greasy bar food, as well, since I didn't eat dinner. What do you recommend?"

"Cooper's is famous for its beer-battered fries, and I can personally vouch for them. The servings are pretty generous. Do you want to split a basket? I'm afraid they don't have much by way of other vegetarian offerings."

"That sounds great. Tonight's on me, though." Nalini insisted on accompanying Lauren to the bar and whipped out her credit card before Lauren could protest. They returned to their table with their drinks.

Nalini tilted her head as Lauren took a sip of her diet cola. "Designated driver?"

Lauren's cheeks flushed. "Actually, I don't drink now. Ever since Luke..."

"Of course." Nalini squeezed Lauren's hand. "I totally understand." She slapped her other hand to her forehead. "Sorry. Does it bother you that I'm drinking?"

Lauren shook her head. "No. I'm used to it by now."

Nalini glanced at the stage, then realized she was still holding Lauren's hand. She let it go reluctantly.

It wasn't long before their fries arrived, and Nalini's eyes grew wide as the waitress set the basket down between them. "You were right. This is a huge serving." She picked one, dunked in it some ketchup, and took a bite. "Mmm...this is amazing."

The pile of fries shrank rapidly as Nalini realized she was hungrier than she thought. She stole a glance at Lauren as she licked ketchup off one finger. Nalini couldn't help focusing on Lauren's lips, and the sensations evoked by that furtive kiss a few days earlier. It hung like an invisible cloud between them, and Nalini knew she'd have to address it sooner or later.

She decided sooner was better and leaned forward. "Lauren...about the other—"

Just then, the speakers at the far end of the room blared to life, and the band did a final sound check. Nalini sat back and sipped her drink, deciding she'd have to wait until a more opportune moment. She couldn't decide if she was relieved or disappointed.

In a few minutes, Josh stepped up to the mike and welcomed their audience.

As Nalini joined in the polite applause that rippled through the small gathering, Josh looked directly at her. He gave her a wink.

"Ladies and gentlemen, our first song is for the two beautiful young ladies over there." Josh waved a hand in their direction, and the band launched into the opening bars of "More Than a Feeling."

Nalini gasped and pulled Lauren close. "You told him?" She had to yell to be heard.

A sly grin spread across Lauren's face. "I may have said something yesterday."

The music swelled, and Nalini closed her eyes. The song brought back memories of when she'd listened to her friend Ravi's playlist, alone in a dorm room surrounded by boxes. It had provided a connection, although a tenuous one, to her former life at a time when she'd been both terrified and exhilarated at the prospect of beginning a new chapter in an as yet unfamiliar country.

When the last few notes faded, Nalini opened her eyes to see Lauren looking directly at her. Both of them applauded with enthusiasm, but Lauren didn't take her eyes off Nalini the entire time.

"They're pretty good," Nalini said at last, taking a long sip from her glass and breaking the spell. "I can see why you like them. Do they do a lot of classic rock covers?"

"Mostly. I really like some of Josh's original songs, but he doesn't play them all that often. Classic rock is one of those guilty pleasures we share, and it always seems to be received well by their audience."

Nalini's lips quirked. "I guess I can't hope for any Harry Styles covers, then?"

Lauren's face went blank. "Harry who?"

"You don't know who Harry Styles is?" Nalini was about to launch into a tirade when she saw the twinkle in Lauren's eyes, and then the two of them burst out laughing at the same time. Nalini picked up an extra crispy fry and flung it at Lauren, who caught it easily with one hand and popped it into her mouth.

They reached into the basket simultaneously, and Lauren's fingers brushed against Nalini's, sending a jolt of electricity through her body. The light from the stage transformed Lauren's hair into a blonde halo, and Nalini was mesmerized, unable to look away.

Whatever Nalini felt for Lauren, it already seemed different from the casual relationships she'd had at Wellesley. After the last one had ended shortly before graduation, Nalini had told herself that getting into another serious relationship was impossible. At the time, her parents had increased the pressure on her to get married, and although Nalini had bought some time, she was all too aware that she'd face an uncomfortable choice in the near future.

Because of that decision, she'd vowed not to get serious with any woman.

And yet, from the first moment she'd seen Lauren in the bookstore, Nalini had realized that she'd have to guard her feelings more than ever. Sex with Lauren would be amazing. Nalini had no doubt of that, even before that fleeting moment of ecstasy when they'd kissed. The question was, would they be able to stop at just sex?

When the waitress walked by, Nalini ordered another Long Island. Tonight, she would just let herself enjoy the music and Lauren's company. That was all.

ELEVEN

LAUREN LEANED ACROSS the table to make herself heard. "Are you having a good time?" The jasmine and coconut notes of Nalini's shampoo teased her senses, and she swallowed, fighting the urge to run her hands through Nalini's lustrous hair.

Nalini, on her third Long Island, grinned. "I'm having a great time. Thank you for inviting me."

When the band took a break, Josh came over and pulled up an empty chair from an adjacent table. He smiled at Nalini. "What do you think of the band?"

"You guys are good. Really good. You should have a record contract by now."

Josh mopped at his forehead. "Well, that's kind of the plan. I've actually been checking into a few indie labels, but we haven't had any luck so far." He wiggled his eyebrows at Nalini. "Now, maybe if we had a drop-dead gorgeous female lead singer..."

Lauren snorted and punched Josh's arm. "Hey, what am I? Chopped liver?"

Josh laughed. "No offense, Lauren, but I've heard you sing. What about it, Nalini?"

A smile hovered on Nalini's lips, and Lauren's knees went weak. It was a good thing she was sitting down.

"Honestly, I don't think I'd do your band any good at all. Besides, Lauren's the classic rock buff."

Josh chatted with them for a few more minutes, but Lauren only had eyes for Nalini. She thought back to when she and Kelly had started dating. It had been good, back then, but no woman had ever made Lauren feel quite like this. And they hadn't even slept together yet.

"Well, I'd better get back to the guys." Josh pushed his chair back and stood up. "Hope you enjoy the second set."

The audience's enthusiasm grew stronger during the second set, no doubt fueled by the additional rounds of drinks that kept the two waitresses busy as they shuttled back and forth among the tables and the bar. Lauren derived just as much enjoyment from the music as she did from watching Nalini's reactions to it. When Josh announced that the band was going to perform one of their original songs, Nalini's eyes lit up, and she applauded along with the rest of the crowd.

The song was one Lauren had heard several times before. She didn't tell Nalini that she'd helped Josh write it, a few months after her brother's death. It was a bittersweet tune, and her eyes filled with tears. She dabbed at them with a napkin, hoping Nalini hadn't noticed.

"I loved it," Nalini said, when the applause died down. She leaned her arm on the back of Lauren's chair, and her lips brushed against Lauren's ear. "They really should do more of their own songs."

An hour later, the band wound down their set, after doing two encores. Lauren checked the time on her phone. She didn't want this night to end, but she knew they both had an early day coming up.

"Would you like to head back?"

Nalini finished the last of her drink. "Not really, but I suppose we should. I had a wonderful evening."

"I'm glad." Lauren pressed her hand against the small of Nalini's back, steering her through the maze of tables and inebriated patrons until they reached the exit.

When they reached the car, Nalini placed a hand on Lauren's shoulder.

"Lauren, before we leave...about the other night..."

Lauren's stomach lurched. "Don't worry. Gone and forgotten."

Nalini sighed. "See, that's just the thing. I can't stop thinking about it." Nalini leaned in, and Lauren instinctively licked her lips. "What I said about not getting involved in a serious relationship...I meant it. I'm not ready for a relationship. But it's driving me crazy, the way I want you. I know it doesn't make any sense to you, but—"

Moving closer, Lauren placed a finger on Nalini's lips. "It does make sense. Look, let's get you back to your dorm. We can talk about it later, okay?"

Lauren's mouth went dry, and she wished she'd had another soda before they'd left the bar. Nalini's words had opened a window of possibility that Lauren had considered might be closed forever. Her heart pounded as she turned the key in the ignition. Could this really work? Could they have a physical relationship with no strings attached, as Nalini had clearly wanted, and still remain just friends?

They remained silent during the drive back to campus, except for Nalini occasionally humming snatches of the songs that the band had played. Lauren stared straight ahead until she pulled up in front of Jorgensen Hall.

She took a deep breath. "Well, here we are." Her palms were sweaty as she released her grip on the wheel.

Nalini unbuckled her seat belt. "Lauren, I mean what I said earlier about wanting you. Would you like to come up?" She moved closer, and Lauren's foot jittered on the floor. There it was again, that intoxicating scent. "I can show you the lavish facilities that we grad students live in."

"I'd...better not." Suddenly, Lauren was very conscious of how warm the night air was.

"Okay. I guess this is good night, then. I really did have a wonderful time." Nalini pressed her palm against Lauren's cheek.

Lauren turned and pulled Nalini to her. When their lips met, the last trace of her hesitation vanished. She kissed Nalini with a yearning she hadn't felt in a long while.

They separated an eternity later. Lauren struggled to breathe, her chest heaving with the effort. "Wow. Is that offer to see your room still available?"

Nalini giggled. "Of course. There's guest parking spots on that side of the building." She pointed to the far end of the lot.

Moments later, they were waiting for the elevator. As soon as they entered, Lauren grabbed Nalini and pulled her close once more. Her lips crushed Nalini's as the elevator doors closed, and her tongue slid between Nalini's lips, drawing a soft moan from Nalini's throat.

Lauren's hand slid around Nalini's waist, her heart thumping erratically as Nalini pressed against her and their breasts squished together.

The elevator dinged, and they broke apart. Taking Lauren's hand, Nalini led her down the narrow hallway. Nalini fumbled with her keys and finally managed to unlock the door to her room. They staggered inside.

Nalini had barely shut the door when Lauren pushed her up against it. This time, Lauren's hands covered Nalini's breasts before she tasted Nalini's lips again, savoring their warmth and softness. Nalini moaned and arched her back, pushing against Lauren's hands.

"Oh god, Lauren, this feels so good," Nalini whispered, when they both came up for air. "Are you sure this is what you want?"

Lauren didn't hesitate. "Yes, I'm sure."

All Lauren's concerns and doubts that had plagued her for the last few days evaporated in the heat that was building between their bodies. All she wanted, at that moment, was to rip Nalini's clothes off and taste her skin, to feel Nalini's naked body pressed against hers.

"Kiss me again," Nalini whispered, her voice dripping with desire.

Lauren shuddered as their lips made contact. Nalini's hands wrapped around Lauren, pulling her down onto the bed. Lauren ran her hands ran down Nalini's thighs and back up again, fumbling with the zipper of Nalini's jeans.

Nalini undid the first few buttons of Lauren's shirt and slipped her hand inside. As Nalini's thumb brushed across Lauren's nipple through her bra, Nalini raised her knee and pressed it between Lauren's thighs.

Lauren moaned as Nalini's hands slipped inside her bra. The delicious thrill of skin against skin added to the heat suffusing her body. Within a few moments, Nalini had removed Lauren's shirt and bra. Nalini's warm mouth closed over one of Lauren's nipples, and she bit back a scream of pleasure.

Soon, Nalini transferred her attention to Lauren's other breast. As Nalini's tongue swirled around Lauren's stiffening nipple, Lauren pushed Nalini's sweatshirt up and over her head. Gently, she lowered Nalini's head down onto the pillow, unhooked Nalini's bra, and nestled her face between Nalini's breasts, taking deep breaths.

The scent of Nalini's skin was intoxicating, adding fuel to the flames already consuming Lauren. Many months of being denied this pleasure had culminated in a hunger unlike any that Lauren had known. She smothered Nalini's breasts with soft kisses, and Nalini whimpered in response.

As Nalini's breathing speeded up, Lauren finally unzipped Nalini's jeans. She slid her hand inside Nalini's underwear, seeking the source of the heat that radiated between Nalini's thighs.

Nalini gasped and bucked her hips when Lauren slipped two fingers inside her.

"Oh god, yes!" Nalini's lips parted, and Lauren bent over her to plant a kiss on them. Lauren's fingers worked faster, and Nalini cried out. Their eyes locked, and Lauren pressed her thumb against the swollen bud of Nalini's clit. As Lauren stroked faster, Nalini pulled Lauren's head down and devoured her lips. The incredible sensations of watching Nalini's face contort with pleasure, feeling Nalini tremble under her touch, and the warmth and wetness engulfing her fingers made Lauren moan. She thrust deeper, curling her fingers as their tongues dueled. At last, Nalini cried out again, her voice muffled by Lauren's lips. Her entire body shook as she came.

By now, Lauren's need had grown urgent. Fortunately, Nalini appeared to know exactly what to do next. Within moments, Nalini had shed her underwear and dispensed with Lauren's clothes as well.

They lay against each other, kissing with an intensity that ramped up as Nalini slipped a hand between Lauren's legs.

"I'm so glad you asked me up," Lauren said, her voice thick with lust.

Nalini sighed. Her hand cupped Lauren's mound, squeezing gently. Then, as Lauren waited, Nalini's fingers explored the source of Lauren's wetness. When two fingers entered her at last, Lauren did her best not to scream.

"Yes, fuck me," she said, gasping. "I want you so much."

With a steady rhythm, Nalini thrust into Lauren over and over again, until Lauren's whole body convulsed with pleasure. Her muscles clamped down around Nalini's fingers.

Nalini moved closer and began to suck on a stiff nipple while she kept up the pace of her thrusts. Then, with a wicked grin, she pressed down on Lauren's clit with her thumb.

The renewed desire in Nalini's eyes finally pushed Lauren over the edge. She arched her back and squeezed her eyes shut, whimpering as she surrendered to the explosive force of her orgasm.

When the dizzying sensation faded, Lauren opened her eyes to see Nalini gazing at her with a hunger that sent a thrill through Lauren all over again.

"That was simply amazing," Nalini said. She kissed Lauren's shoulder. "Seeing you come like that almost made me come again."

Lauren held Nalini close, still unable to speak. Gradually, her breathing slowed to a normal rate.

"I really needed that," Lauren whispered.

"Do you want to stay here tonight?"

A pang of regret stabbed at Lauren's chest. "I'd love to, but I have to get back home. I'd rather not have to explain things to my mom just yet."

Nalini raised herself on one elbow. "So, are we still friends?"

"Of course." Lauren's breath caught in her throat. The earlier uncertainty started to return, but she pushed it aside once more. "I know you said you didn't want a relationship, but let's just enjoy the way things are for now, without overthinking it." Lauren knew that they were already venturing into dangerous territory but, right now, her body and her brain were sending two different sets of signals.

Nalini's fingers brushed against Lauren's cheek. "I'd like that. Does that make us friends with benefits? I've never really thought about that before, but it seems like it would be an appropriate description in this case."

With her heart thumping, Lauren kissed Nalini again and then sat up. "You have a deal."

TWELVE

NALINI ARRIVED AT the designated classroom for her first review session well ahead of time, and she had to wait outside for several minutes while the previous class finished up. She was grateful for the opportunity to calm her nerves, taking slow, steady breaths. She stole a few discreet glances at the handful of students gathered in the hallway.

She'd barely made it to her first class on time that morning after sleeping through her alarm. The night with Lauren was all she could think of as she'd taken a quick detour through the Student Union cafeteria and grabbed a cup of coffee and a granola bar for breakfast. Sex with Lauren had been better than she'd ever imagined, and Nalini still couldn't completely shake the idea that it had all been a dream.

After Lauren had left, Nalini had stayed awake for a while, replaying the time they'd shared together in her head. The intensity of Lauren's passion had both surprised and thrilled her. Maybe it was because Nalini hadn't had sex for almost a year, but she couldn't remember the last time she'd been so completely in tune, physically and emotionally, with another woman. Even her last, tumultuous relationship at Wellesley didn't approach the experience she'd had during just one night with Lauren.

Her nerves over her first teaching assignment soon brought her down to reality. After the current class broke up, Nalini waited a moment longer before entering the room and placing her books on the table at the front. It looked like it could hold about forty or fifty students but, according to the enrollment figures she'd received from the department office, she was supposed to have only twenty-five in her class. In the interest of offering the students a more personal experience, the department had broken up the huge freshman biology class into smaller sections for the review sessions.

She glanced at the clock, walked over to the whiteboard, and cleared her throat. This was it. Her body went rigid for a moment as she looked around the classroom.

Nalini had barely introduced herself when one of the students in the back row raised his hand.

"Is this stuff going to be on the test?"

A ripple of laughter spread across the classroom, breaking the tension. Nalini joined in.

"Nobody knows what's going to be on the test except Professor McConnell, and he's not telling. However, from what he's told our group of teaching assistants, students who attend these review sessions regularly tend to get better grades than those who don't."

Another hand went up, a girl this time. "You mean we don't have to attend these sessions if we don't want to?"

Nalini suppressed a sigh. Professor McConnell had warned her that some of the students would drop out in the first couple of weeks, but he believed in letting students make their own choices.

"No, they're not mandatory. As I said, it does help if you want to make progress with the class, but you're free to attend or not, as you please. In fact, if any of you would rather not be here, you can leave now."

Silence fell over the room like a thick winter blanket. The students exchanged uneasy glances with one another, and then three of them picked up their backpacks and walked out the door. Nalini noted, with interest, that the boy who had questioned her earlier had remained seated.

"Good. Now that we've got things cleared up, let's get started." She picked up a marker.

Once Nalini got into the rhythm of the lesson, her nerves settled down, and she actually began to enjoy herself. For the most part, the students seemed to be paying attention, and some of them even asked reasonable questions as the class went along.

It was only when she'd dismissed the students, fifty minutes later, that thoughts of Lauren returned. Thankfully, the review session was her last class of the afternoon. Nalini headed back to her dorm, looking forward to an early dinner and, maybe, spending some more time with Lauren later.

She was disappointed that Lauren hadn't texted her since their night of shared bliss. Not wanting to seem too pushy, Nalini hadn't made any attempt to get in touch with Lauren either, as much as she'd longed to. She walked across campus, her head down and lost in thought, until she heard a familiar voice calling her name.

Nalini turned around to see Emi smiling and waving at her.

"Okay if I walk with you?"

Nalini nodded, suddenly glad for the distraction. "I'd like that."

"How's your week going?"

Nalini sighed. "Busy. I already have two assignments due next week."

"I know what you mean. I really wish I could get started on a research program, but my class schedule is pretty full."

"Tell me about it. I think they do that deliberately, to torture us in our first semester, so they can screen out the wimps. I heard several grad students dropped out of last year's class after their first semester."

Emi laughed. "That must be it. So, do you have big plans for the weekend?"

"Not really. I was going to check in with a…a friend later, but I'm afraid I'll be spending most of my time working on those assignments. How about you?"

"Nothing big. One of my classmates who lives off campus is throwing a party Saturday night. You should come and have a night of fun, so you don't spend your entire weekend working on assignments. I already invited a couple of other people from Jorgensen. Actually, this one guy sort of invited himself. I met him in the kitchenette yesterday, when I was having dinner. I'm not really sure about him. He tends to come on a little strong."

Once glance at Emi's expression told Nalini what she needed to know. A bubble of laughter rose in her throat. "Let me guess. His name is Paul, right?"

Emi's lips formed a perfect O. "How did you know?"

"We've met. Actually, he's the first person I met in Jorgensen."

In a short while, after animated discussions that revolved around Paul's taste in women and music, they reached the entrance to Jorgensen Hall. Nalini and Emi exchanged phone numbers, and Nalini promised to let Emi know if she could make it to the party. She wondered if Lauren would like to go with her.

Should she wait for Lauren to text her first? For a while, Nalini felt like she was in grade school again, back in Mumbai, in the throes of her first schoolgirl crush.

"To hell with it," she muttered and pulled out her phone.

Would you like to go to a party Saturday night? It'll probably be a bunch of boring grad students, but if you're not doing anything…

It was over an hour later—an hour of Nalini wringing her hands, pacing up and down her room, and eventually flopping down on her bed with a book—before her phone pinged.

Sorry…really busy night at the bookstore. Yes, that sounds great.

As Nalini prepared to compose her response, another message came in.

I've missed you.

Nalini's hands trembled as she typed. *Missed you, too.*

She put down her phone after agreeing on a time to meet and returned to the novel she was reading. However, after several minutes of staring at the same page over and over again, she closed the book.

Lauren had missed her. Worse, Nalini had admitted to doing the same thing. Was that crossing an invisible line? Somehow, Nalini didn't think friends with benefits were supposed to miss each other when they hadn't been together for just a few days. Or, at least, they weren't supposed to admit it. Was she simply reading too much into Lauren's willingness to go to the party?

She groaned. This was already getting complicated. She'd have to tread carefully.

After a few more futile attempts to read, Nalini gave up. The memories of her night with Lauren, which she'd managed to push aside to some extent, had now returned in full force, thanks to their brief text conversation. The feeling of Lauren's warm breath on her skin, Lauren's kisses on her nipples, and Lauren's fingers penetrating her, propelling her toward blissful release, wiped everything else from Nalini's mind.

Although she'd planned to head to the cafeteria for dinner, Nalini realized she had a more urgent hunger that demanded to be satisfied first. She reached into her drawer for her vibrator, thankful that she'd remembered to bring it with her. It had been the result of a clandestine shopping trip in Boston, with a few giggling classmates, for her first birthday at Wellesley.

Whispering Lauren's name and picturing Lauren's tongue taking her to ever-greater heights of pleasure, Nalini came within a few minutes. She cleaned up the vibrator, put it away, and got dressed again. Her knees were still wobbly when she left her room.

THIRTEEN

L AUREN PICKED UP the pile of paperbacks that had fallen on the floor, a not infrequent occurrence after a busy morning at the store. After she had reshelved them, her gaze fell on a book titled *Friends with Benefits*.

She picked it up and skimmed the synopsis on the back. She didn't normally read straight romances, but she wondered if she should start. Maybe the book would give her some clues about her relationship with Nalini.

Lauren understood Nalini's desire not to get involved in a serious relationship. A couple of years ago, Lauren had felt the same way. After her tumultuous relationship with Kelly had ended, Lauren should have been the last person in the world to want anything long-term.

"Hey, Lauren, can you give me a hand?" Chelsea's voice broke into Lauren's thoughts, and she quickly returned the book to its shelf.

"Be right there."

Lauren was glad that Jen had found a replacement for Sonia so quickly. Although Lauren missed Sonia, Chelsea was proving to be a capable employee. A few weeks before Sonia was due to leave, Lauren had discussed taking on extra hours until Jen hired a replacement. She wasn't thrilled by the prospect of longer hours, but the extra cash would have been helpful. As it turned out, they'd had several applicants within hours of Jen posting the position on the bookstore's social media channels. Chelsea had graduated recently from the University of Southern Maine in Portland and had moved back in with her parents in Zachary. For now, she was willing to work part time. Both Jen and Lauren had liked her easy-going manner and sense of humor when she'd interviewed for the job.

Lauren made her way to the front of the store. A woman stood at the counter, tapping her fingers, while Chelsea frowned at the iPad that served as the mobile interface to the store's point-of-sale system. "What's up?"

Chelsea shot Lauren a grateful look. "I haven't yet figured out how to do a preorder. I know Jen was going to show me today, but she's been in her office all evening with the accountant."

"No problem. It's really easy...when you know how, of course."

With a few taps on the screen, Lauren guided Chelsea through the process. The customer walked away satisfied, knowing that a copy of her favorite author's latest book would be set aside for her as soon as it arrived.

The store grew busier over the next hour, and Lauren had little time to think about Nalini. She even decided to skip her evening break. With Jen still occupied in her closet-sized office, Lauren didn't want to leave Chelsea to handle the counter alone.

While Lauren was helping a customer find a particularly obscure book in the science fiction section, her phone buzzed with a text. Jen didn't mind her employees using cell phones while they worked, but Lauren always silenced hers. She decided the message could wait for the moment.

After helping another customer check out, Lauren glanced at the door to Jen's office as it opened. Deanna, the bookstore's accountant, stepped out. Lauren had met Deanna on just a couple of occasions, and she gave the older woman a brief smile. Lauren sucked in a breath as Jen followed. Jen's face had drained of all color, making her mane of curly red hair seem even more fiery by contrast. Lauren was about to say something, but Jen escorted

Deanna to the door and stepped outside. Lauren's eyes narrowed as they hugged briefly.

Chelsea nudged Lauren. "What's going on?"

"I don't know. I hope she's okay."

A few minutes later, Jen returned. Her face wasn't as pale as before, but she was wringing her hands.

"Can you two manage without me for a while longer? I'll be in my office." Jen began to walk away without waiting for an answer.

"Of course. Jen, is everything okay?" Lauren followed her and placed a hand on Jen's arm.

"I'm fine. If you and Chelsea have a few moments, can we get together after closing? I'm sure things will slow down tonight, so if you want to close a bit early, that's fine with me."

Lauren decided not to press the issue. She nodded and walked back to the counter.

Chelsea moved a pile of books behind the counter and dusted off her hands. "I know I haven't been here long, and I don't know Jen all that well, but she seemed really upset."

"I guess we'll find out." Lauren looked up as the bell over the front door clanged. The stream of Friday night visitors to the store continued for the next hour, but as it grew closer to closing time, only two customers were left browsing the stacks.

"I think we can close up after those two leave," Lauren whispered to Chelsea. "We still have a half-hour to go, but I don't expect we'll get any more customers now."

Chelsea nodded. "Sounds good to me."

After their last customer had left, Lauren locked the door and flipped the sign over. While Chelsea completed the rest of their daily closing ritual, Lauren knocked on Jen's door.

"We're closing now."

"Thanks. I'll be out in a minute." Jen was looking better than she had earlier, but Lauren could tell she wasn't her usual self. Her face had regained its color, but her fleeting smile was devoid of its usual warmth.

A short while later, Jen joined them at the counter. "Thank you for giving me some time to think through this. There's no easy way to put this, so I won't bother telling you all the analysis that's been running through my head this evening. The fact is, the store isn't doing as well as I thought. If we don't turn things around by the end of the year, I'll have to reduce our hours or consider shutting down completely."

Lauren gasped. The world that she'd known for the past several years was suddenly spinning out of control. "But...it seemed like we were pretty busy this summer. How is this happening?"

Jen sighed. "I'm not sure. I thought our sales were flat this year, but it turns out that our net revenue has actually been declining. There are several factors that may have contributed to it, and it's certainly not a unique problem. A lot of independent bookstores, and even the chain stores, are facing this problem. It's true that we've had the same customer traffic we did last year, but it appears that more people are browsing and less are buying. Or, at least, they're not buying physical books anymore."

Jen turned to Chelsea. "I know this looks particularly bad to you, Chelsea, and I'm sorry I had to dump this on you in your first week. However, please rest assured that I'm not going to cut hours yet, either for you or Lauren. In fact, that's the last thing I want to do, as it will only hurt our sales more at this point. I'm working on some ideas for boosting sales, but it will take time."

Lauren's head was still spinning when she left the store and got into her car. She'd suspected things weren't going well with the store for some time, but she hadn't wanted to raise the issue with Jen. The market had been changing, and Lauren sometimes felt that trying to maintain the bookstore as it had been for the past fifty years or so would no longer be the best strategy.

Although it didn't pay much more than working in retail, which was Lauren's other option when she'd moved back to Zachary, Lauren enjoyed her job. Being surrounded by books and discussing them with customers all day long fed her soul. She still remembered the agony of filling out job applications at department stores, a gas station, and even at the grocery store where her mother worked, knowing those jobs would never be anything more than a paycheck. She'd considered herself fortunate that Jen had been hiring at the time. Given Lauren's passion for reading, it had seemed like the perfect match, although she had never considered it a career.

Now, Lauren began to wonder if it was time to fill out another application at Hudson's. Maybe her mother could put in a word with Dave.

As she pulled out of the alley behind the store, Lauren shook her head. She couldn't abandon Jen now. She would see this through, no matter what happened.

When Lauren started her shift the next morning, she was relieved to find Jen in a more upbeat mood. The dark circles under Jen's eyes compelled Lauren to give her a hug as soon as she walked in the door. Other than the lack of sleep—possibly the reason she was drinking an extra tall cup of Fleischmann's coffee instead of her usual twelve-ounce—the old Jen was back.

"The first thing I'm planning to do is hold some more local events, like book clubs and signings," Jen said. "I know I've been reluctant to organize things like that in the past, but they do bring in more traffic to the store."

Lauren put her arm around Jen's shoulders. "I'll do whatever I can to help. Just tell me what you need."

"I'm going to start by taking up an old friend of mine on her offer. Have you heard of Alyssa Forester?"

Lauren's jaw dropped. "You know Alyssa Forester?" Although Lauren hadn't read any of Forester's books, which were all straight romances, she knew enough to remember that some of them had made both the *New York Times* and *USA Today* bestseller lists, a rare distinction for a self-published author. Her eight contemporary romance series occupied prime real estate in the store, making them the lone exception to Jen's policy of not stocking self-published books. Since self-published paperbacks were nonreturnable, Jen had explained to Lauren that she only stocked big names that were guaranteed to sell. Now Lauren knew why Forester had made that select list. Lauren wondered if she would be able to get her own books into a store. That is, if she ever finished a novel and published it.

"We were in the same writers' group when I lived in Portland," Jen said. "Of course, that was long before she became famous, but we've kept in touch since then. I'd talked to her earlier this year, to congratulate her on her latest award, and she'd mentioned the possibility of doing a signing here."

"That would be awesome." Secretly, Lauren wished that Jen had managed to invite one of her favorite lesbian romance authors instead, but that was unlikely to ever happen in a small town like Zachary. The potential audience for lesbian romance novels was far too small. Besides, she doubted an Australian author would bother making the trip to a small Maine bookstore just to do a signing.

Jen outlined other ideas for ramping up sales and changing the store's inventory, so they could cater to student interests as well as their seasonal clientele. By the time Lauren finished her shift that afternoon, she was feeling considerably better about her future employment status. And, in a less than a day, she'd be seeing Nalini. Lauren's partying days had pretty much ended after she left Orono, and she wasn't big on large social gatherings, especially with people she didn't know. But she'd get to spend some time with Nalini, and that prospect alone had tempted her to accept Nalini's invitation the night before. As much as Lauren tried not to admit it to herself, the thought of seeing Nalini again accounted for a good portion of her upbeat mood.

FOURTEEN

NALINI FOUGHT AN urge to pull Lauren into her arms for a kiss when Lauren drove up to the entrance of Jorgensen Hall on Saturday night. Instead, she slipped into the seat beside Lauren and looked up the address on her phone, then handed it to Lauren.

She still wasn't sure exactly where things stood between them. When she hadn't heard from Lauren for several days before finally texting Lauren about the party, she had begun to wonder if Lauren was having second thoughts about their arrangement. And yet, the unmistakable hunger in Lauren's eyes now told Nalini a different story. Maybe that kiss wouldn't have been such a bad idea after all.

"Pull over here for a minute," Nalini said, as they turned onto the campus loop.

Lauren raised her eyebrows but did as Nalini requested. "Are you all right? Do you need to get out, or—"

Nalini's hands wrapped around Lauren's shoulders, and she tasted the sweet softness of Lauren's lips. After a moment's hesitation, Lauren parted her lips. Her soft moan thrilled Nalini, and her tongue darted into Nalini's mouth.

They broke apart, gasping.

"I guess that was a good reason for pulling over." Lauren brushed her lips with the back of her hand. "I really did miss you."

"When you hadn't got in touch after...well, after that night, I was afraid you'd changed your mind. About us, I mean."

Lauren looked away. "To be honest, I was confused. I thought it was best not to say anything until I worked things out."

"And have you worked things out?" Nalini rested a hand on Lauren's thigh.

Lauren turned back to Nalini, a smile playing across her lips. She moved closer and crushed Nalini's lips under hers. "Does that tell you anything?"

Nalini leaned back against her seat. Her heart was thumping so loud, she was sure Lauren could hear it. "I suppose I can accept that answer. Now, we should probably get going to this party."

Lauren chuckled and eased the car out into the street again.

The house was only a few minutes away from campus, and Lauren knew the neighborhood well. "It's a popular neighborhood for students," she told Nalini as she parked the car. "The locals tend to stay away, and the houses here are mostly rentals."

The relentless, bone-rattling thump of music and sounds of laughter filtered through the windows as they walked up the driveway. Nalini hoped someone she knew would be there. It did seem a little weird to be walking into a stranger's house with a guest who didn't know anyone there, either. Fortunately, as they wandered in through the open door, she spotted Emi and waved.

"I'm so glad you could make it." Emi gave Nalini a hug and glanced from her to Lauren.

"This is my friend Lauren," Nalini said, noticing the look. "She works at the bookstore in town. Lauren, this is Emi, a grad student who's also in Jorgensen."

They shook hands, and Emi pointed them in the direction of the keg. It was near the doorway of a box-like kitchen off the living room, which was already filled with people.

"I'll get you a soda," Nalini told Lauren as they wound their way through the press of bodies. "This reminds me of my freshman year at Wellesley. It's been a while since I went to a kegger."

Lauren took the can of diet cola from Nalini, and their fingers met for a brief, delicious moment. It was enough to make Nalini's entire body ache with longing for more of Lauren's touch.

"My freshman year in Orono wasn't that different." Lauren opened the can and raised it to her lips. "And my sophomore year, to be fair. When I wasn't out at parties like this, I was bar-hopping with my friends."

"I know bars don't bother you now, but is it difficult being at parties with everyone drinking?" A brief twinge of guilt made Nalini stare at the foam in her cup.

Lauren shrugged. "Not really. Actually, I rarely go to parties these days, so it's not much of an issue."

Nalini took a sip from her plastic cup, and they edged past a couple of students into the living room.

"Hey, look who's here! The most beautiful woman on campus."

Nalini spun around as a hand landed on her shoulder. "Oh—hi, Paul." She shot a warning glance at Lauren, who seemed to be having considerable difficulty hiding her smirk. "This is my...friend, Lauren. Lauren, I may have mentioned Paul. He's another grad student from my dorm. We're probably in a minority here, though. This is mostly an undergrad crowd, so I guess the word must have spread. I do believe our hosts are grad students, but I haven't met them yet."

Paul shook Lauren's hand. "So which program are you in, Lauren? Not in physics, I'm sure. I would have noticed you at once. And I'll have to amend my earlier statement. I'm now standing here with the *two* most beautiful women on campus."

Lauren bit her lip. "Actually, I'm not a student. I work in town. But thank you, anyway."

"Fascinating. You must tell me all about this thing called work." Paul linked an arm through Lauren's and led her across the room. Nalini followed, grinning, until she spotted a student in the biology class she was teaching who waved at her. Nalini glanced at Lauren, who appeared to be holding her own with Paul, and walked over to the cluster of students.

By the time Nalini looked for Lauren again, she discovered that both Lauren and Paul were in the same spot where she'd left them a half hour earlier, in a corner of the room. She stopped to refill her cup in the kitchen before joining them.

Paul looked at Nalini and grinned. "I should have known you two were together the moment I walked in."

Nalini laughed. "We're friends, that's all."

Paul's eyebrows shot up. "Just friends? Well, I need a refill. All that talking made me thirsty, I guess." He winked at Lauren. "Lauren is such a good listener. Can I get you ladies anything?"

They both declined, and Paul vanished into the crowd.

"He's a really nice guy, when you can get him to stop talking about theoretical physics." Lauren brushed back a strand of Nalini's hair that had fallen across her forehead.

"I'm sorry I abandoned you."

Lauren waved a hand. "It was fine, really. I do like Paul. And, honestly, I didn't say anything about us being together. I just told him we met at the bookstore."

Nalini wasn't sure if it was the cheap beer—two cups were barely enough to give her a buzz—but she found Lauren's hypnotic blue eyes even more irresistible than usual. She allowed herself to get lost in them for a short while. "So...we *are* just friends, aren't we?"

"Isn't that what you wanted?" Lauren frowned.

Just as Nalini was about to reply, Emi clapped her on the shoulder. "Having a good time?"

"Yeah, thanks for inviting me."

Emi engaged Lauren in conversation about her job at Great Expectations, and it turned out that they shared a common interest in Victorian literature. Still thinking about Lauren's question, Nalini only half-listened as Lauren discussed Dickens with Emi, her eyes flashing while she expounded on one of her favorite subjects. The more Nalini thought about her relationship with Lauren, the more she realized that keeping things uncomplicated wasn't going to be as easy as she'd thought at first.

What did Lauren mean to her, really? From the start, Nalini had known this wasn't going to be another casual affair, like the ones she'd had at Wellesley. Lauren was different. Lauren already meant more to Nalini than her previous lovers, even before Lauren ended up in her bed that one memorable night. And that was exactly why Nalini was afraid of their relationship progressing beyond its current stage.

"Hey, wanna dance?"

Nalini turned to see a tall, skinny guy lurch toward her, clinging to a cup with an unsteady hand. His close-cropped blond hair still managed to look untidy, and his Metallica T shirt had definitely seen better days.

"Um, no thanks." She sipped her beer and moved closer to Lauren and Emi.

"Aw, come on." He grabbed her wrist. "I won't bite. I promise."

"Let go of me." Nalini's voice cut through the buzz of conversation around them. "I said no."

Metallica shirt guy scowled but maintained his grip on her wrist. "What are you, like, a lesbian or something?" He pulled her closer.

Almost with a reflexive gesture, Nalini lifted her cup and flung the contents into his face.

He howled with rage and pawed at his eyes.

"Leave her alone, Mike."

Nalini, her hand still trembling, turned to see Paul standing behind her. He brushed past her and grabbed Mike's shoulder. "Come on. You've had enough to drink. Let's go outside."

As Nalini watched, her chest heaving with the effort to breathe, Paul led the drunk toward a door. Nalini's gaze followed them as she took several deep breaths.

"Are you okay?" Lauren took Nalini's hand in her own.

Nalini nodded. "I'm fine. Just a bit shaken up, that's all."

"God, Nalini, I'm so sorry." Emi's delicate features were etched with concern. "I have no idea who that creep was."

"It's not your fault." The warmth of Lauren's hand was already soothing Nalini's frayed nerves. "I owe Paul a favor, though."

Emi sighed. "You know, I've been revising my opinion of Paul tonight. I actually spent quite some time talking to him earlier. He's not so bad once you get to know him."

Nalini managed a weak grin. "I'm glad he was here."

After Emi apologized again, she drifted over to a group of her classmates, and Nalini was alone with Lauren once more.

Lauren leaned closer, and the subtle citrus scent of her perfume made Nalini's pulse race. "Do you want to get out of here?"

"Yes, let's." Nalini looked around for Emi, but she'd vanished already. They walked down a hallway past the crowded kitchen and out the back door of the house.

The cool air was a welcome relief, and Nalini began to feel better as they walked down the street to Lauren's car. Although she was glad to be away from the noise of the party, Nalini didn't want the night to end.

"I like your friend Emi," Lauren said, breaking the silence as she unlocked her car. "She has good taste in literature. Are you ready to head back to your dorm?"

Nalini looked into the blue depths of Lauren's eyes, and her stomach fluttered. Her earlier resolve to maintain a safe distance melted away. Suddenly, the question of their relationship didn't matter as much. "Only if you promise to come up with me. And spend the night this time."

Lauren held her gaze for what seemed like several minutes. "I guess I could text my mom and let her know I'm going to crash at a friend's place tonight, just so she doesn't panic in the morning. She already knows about the party."

"Is that a yes?" Nalini's fingers brushed against Lauren's cheek. Heat coiled in her belly.

Lauren grasped Nalini's hand and held it against her cheek for a moment, before bringing it to her lips. "That's a yes."

FIFTEEN

UNLIKE LAUREN'S PREVIOUS visit to Nalini's dorm, this one was more relaxed. There was no frenzied groping in the elevator, just the two of them holding hands, and a building sense of anticipation that Lauren enjoyed. Her desire for Nalini hadn't changed, but it was more measured now that she knew they had the whole night ahead of them.

Apparently, Nalini felt the same way. When the door to her room closed behind them, she gave Lauren a tender, unhurried kiss before leading her to the bed. The bed that they'd be sharing.

"It's not as spacious as your house, but I'll do my best to make it up to you." Nalini must have noticed Lauren checking out the bed. "I do have a couple of unopened toothbrushes, in case you're wondering," Nalini said, as she stretched. She removed her sweatshirt and tossed it onto the floor. "And you can borrow one of my T shirts to sleep in. Unless you prefer to sleep naked, of course."

"That depends. Do you think we'll be doing much sleeping?" Lauren reached for Nalini's hand and pulled her close. Their lips crashed together, and this time there was no containing the heat that surged through Lauren's body and spilled from every pore. Her tongue slid between Nalini's parted lips.

They fell back onto the bed, lips still locked. Lauren reached under Nalini's T shirt and pulled it up. Her hands explored Nalini's warm skin. When they broke the kiss at last, Lauren wasted no time in removing Nalini's bra.

For a moment, she lay on top of Nalini, transfixed by her sultry beauty. Ever since their previous night together, Lauren had known she'd wanted this more than anything in the world. And yet, she'd held back, afraid that she'd reach the point where she would no longer be able to let Nalini go.

Tonight, though, wasn't about thinking. As she covered the graceful curve of Nalini's neck with kisses, Lauren's hunger grew stronger. She buried her face in Nalini's hair, inhaling the now familiar aroma of coconut and jasmine until it saturated her senses.

Her hands cupped Nalini's breasts, and Nalini moaned. The sound sparked a fresh wave of desire that churned deep within Lauren's belly. She moved lower and ran her tongue in circles around one dusky nipple until it hardened. Nalini gasped and arched her back. Lauren transferred her attention to Nalini's other breast and was rewarded with another low, throaty moan.

"Oh god, I want you," Nalini whispered, her fingers raking Lauren's scalp. "It seems like forever since I felt your kisses on my skin."

Lauren's knee pushed its way between Nalini's thighs. The fabric of Nalini's jeans concealed what Lauren wanted so desperately. With a heavy sigh, Lauren pulled away from Nalini's breasts, pausing only to drink in their beauty once again before she unfastened the button on Nalini's jeans, unzipped them, and then tugged both her jeans and underwear down to her ankles.

Nalini watched Lauren with heavy-lidded eyes, the hunger in them adding to Lauren's own need. Then she sat up and tugged at Lauren's shirt. "It's not fair. You should be naked too."

Before long, Lauren's clothes joined the pile on the floor. She embraced Nalini again, breasts pressing against breasts, legs intertwined, their mutual need growing even stronger. Once more, their lips met. As Lauren devoured Nalini's soft lips, she slid a hand between their bodies and placed it between Nalini's thighs.

Lauren's fingers explored Nalini's wetness until, with a soft moan, she slipped two fingers inside Nalini. Nalini shuddered as Lauren began to thrust in and out. With a gentle shove, she rolled Lauren onto her side.

"I want to fuck you, too," Nalini said. She teased Lauren's tender flesh with one finger before pushing it into Lauren.

Their eyes locked as their fingers moved in unison. Lauren's breathing grew increasingly erratic as Nalini stepped up the pace of her thrusts.

"You're so beautiful," Lauren said, her voice hoarse with the intensity of her longing. Her gaze was drawn to the answering hunger in Nalini's eyes. "I'm glad we're doing this."

"I've been thinking about nothing but this all night." Nalini's eyes grew wider still as Lauren pressed her thumb against Nalini's swollen clit. "Don't stop. Please don't stop."

Nalini's fingers, still buried inside Lauren, went still. Lauren rubbed in tight circles around Nalini's clit, thrilled by the expression on Nalini's face. Her face contorted and a moan burst from her throat. Her entire body went rigid for several moments as she came, and then she relaxed and buried her face in Lauren's shoulder.

"Your turn now." Nalini began to move her fingers again, and Lauren surrendered to the liquid pleasure that was coursing through her veins. This was what Lauren had wanted too, and yet she had been afraid to admit it, most of all to herself. She wished she was more like Nalini, who seemed to have no problems telling Lauren exactly what she wanted.

Nalini's fingers stopped moving, and Lauren whimpered. "Nalini, I need to—"

"I want to taste you."

Lauren lay on her back, and just the sight of Nalini's head buried between her thighs almost made her come right away. She held on to Nalini, and soon Nalini's tongue was teasing her, licking circles around her clit. Over and over again, Nalini's skillful tongue brought Lauren to the edge and left her hanging there, gasping for breath.

Just when Lauren was ready to beg, Nalini flicked her tongue over Lauren's clit and plunged a finger inside her.

Lauren bit back a scream as waves of pleasure washed over her. She came hard, bucking and writhing, hanging on to Nalini's head with both hands until she was completely spent.

"Come here," Lauren whispered, when she was able to breathe normally again.

Nalini climbed over Lauren, a sly grin curling up the corners of her mouth. Lauren kissed her hard, tasting herself on Nalini's lips.

For a while, they lay side by side without speaking. One of Lauren's hands was draped across Nalini's breasts, and Nalini's leg sprawled across Lauren's thighs.

At last, Nalini broke the silence. "That was...incredible."

Lauren couldn't help smiling. "Yes, it was." She turned over and pulled Nalini close. "This is pretty incredible, too. Just being here with you."

Nalini bit her lip. "Lauren, are you sure you're okay with this?"

"The 'friends with benefits' thing?" Lauren brushed a wayward strand of hair away from Nalini's cheek and sighed. "To be honest, I'm not sure. I have to admit the benefits are pretty good."

"But?"

"A few months ago, I would have been fine with this. Actually, after I broke up with Kelly, I had pretty much decided I never wanted to be in a relationship again."

Nalini squeezed Lauren's hand. "What happened?"

Lauren closed her eyes briefly as her chest tightened. "I found out she'd been cheating on me for over a month."

"Oh god, I'm so sorry!" Nalini flung her arms around Lauren's neck and held her close. "I shouldn't have asked," she whispered into Lauren's hair.

"It's okay. I don't mind talking about it now. After that happened, I just didn't think I could trust anyone again."

"I understand." The warmth of Nalini's breath on Lauren's shoulder helped dull the pain that memories of Kelly had reawakened. And yet, Lauren realized, here she was, contemplating a journey down that same road. She decided to move the conversation away from her past.

"What about you? I'm sure you must have broken the hearts of hundreds of Priyanka Chopra fans by now."

Nalini chuckled and punched Lauren's arm. "I did my share of exploring at Wellesley. I mean, there I was, surrounded by women everywhere I went. I figured the odds were pretty good. It was kind of like a lesbian heaven, really. But I didn't let anyone get close enough to even worry about broken hearts."

Lauren raised herself on one elbow and gazed into Nalini's eyes. "So, you're afraid, too."

"It's not that simple."

"Try me."

Nalini heaved a sigh. She traced a finger over Lauren's lips. "It sounds silly, but I don't want a relationship because I know how it's going to end."

"What do you mean?"

"My parents are planning to marry me off to some guy I barely know."

Lauren couldn't believe what she'd just heard. "That's...weird."

"It's not unusual for an Indian woman, even in families who consider themselves more progressive. And my parents are still rather traditional in a lot of ways."

"You can't be serious, though. I mean, this is the rest of your life we're talking about!"

Nalini lowered her gaze. "I know. I'll have to confront them about it sooner or later. My cousin Sanjeev says I usually deal with my problems by running away from them. I suppose he's right."

"Is that why you haven't come out to your parents?" Lauren's mind flashed back to the time she finally admitted to her mother that she wasn't interested in dating boys. Since then, she had come to take her mother's acceptance for granted, but Nalini's predicament made her realize how fortunate she'd been.

"For the most part. It would have the same effect as refusing to marry whoever they've chosen. Worse, actually."

Lauren raised her eyebrows. "What could they do that would be so horrible?"

"Usually, in this situation, your family disowns you. At the very least, I know my parents would cut me off financially. My friend Ravi is still estranged from his parents after coming out several years ago."

"I can't even imagine that happening." Lauren brushed her fingertips against Nalini's cheek. "Don't get me wrong. My family has its share of issues, and I hardly ever hear from my dad these days. I was terrified at first when I decided to come out to my mom. But whatever happened, I never once thought she'd end up kicking me out of the house."

Nalini sighed. "It's a very different culture. Not all Indian parents are as wedded to tradition as mine but, as I said, it's more common than most people realize."

"So, you're just going to go home and...what then? Get married?"

"I...I don't know." Nalini's eyes glistened, and Lauren kissed her cheek. "I haven't decided what to do. I know I'm running out of time. The thing is, my parents financed my entire education at Wellesley, and I know it didn't come cheap. The teaching assistantship covers my tuition here, but I'm still totally dependent on my parents for other expenses. I just can't afford to lose their support."

"Could you get a part-time job, if it came to that?"

"Not on a student visa. I might qualify for work-study, but there aren't many of those positions to go around for international students."

Lauren sat up. The giddy heights of pleasure that she'd experienced just moments ago had been replaced with a sickening ache in the pit of her stomach. "I wish I had a ton of money stashed away, so I could make you my kept woman."

Nalini giggled. "That doesn't sound bad at all. Do you have a rich uncle somewhere?"

"Not in my family, unfortunately."

"Look, let's forget about this for now and just enjoy what we have. I really want to keep seeing you, but I'll understand if you change your mind about our arrangement."

Lauren pulled Nalini into a hug. "Friends with benefits it is. Speaking of benefits..."

She fastened her lips around Nalini's nipple and teased it with her tongue until it stiffened. Nalini sighed with pleasure and pulled Lauren back down onto the bed.

SIXTEEN

S O, WHAT DO you know about Paul?" Emi sipped her coffee, eyeing Nalini's pile of French toast strips liberally doused with maple syrup. Emi had convinced Nalini to join her for a late breakfast at the Student Union cafeteria. To Nalini's surprise, Emi—who had stayed at the party until the early hours of the morning—showed no ill effects, at least as far as her appetite was concerned.

Nalini shrugged. "Probably as much as you do, I guess." She smacked Emi's hand away when Emi attempted to stab a piece of French toast with a fork. "Why do you ask?"

With a glance at her own plate, which was wiped clean, Emi sighed. "I should have got a double serving of the sausage. Maybe I can go back for some." She looked over her shoulder at the serving counters across the hall. "And definitely more French toast."

"That's not an answer." Nalini grimaced. "Oh my god, Emi, are you interested in Paul?"

"I might be." Emi reached over to Nalini's plate again and, this time, Nalini was too slow to react. With a triumphant grin, Emi brought the soggy French toast strip to her mouth. "Oh, this is so good. I really do think I'll go back and get some more food." She stood up. "Can I get you anything?"

Nalini shook her head, then eyed her coffee cup. "Well, maybe some more coffee."

"You got it. I'll be right back."

Nalini couldn't help grinning while she finished the last of her breakfast. Granted, she didn't know that many people on campus as yet, but the idea of Emi and Paul getting together would never have crossed her mind. She liked Paul, and if it worked out between him and Emi, she'd be happy for both of them.

When Emi returned, bearing two coffees and a plate of French toast, Nalini immediately grabbed a piece. "Why don't you just ask Paul out?"

"I don't know." Emi glared at her, but Nalini got the sense it was more about the food than Paul. "I think I should get to know him better. He seems interesting. I hate to admit it, but after talking to him, I've actually started reading this book about string theory. It's pretty cool stuff."

Recalling her first conversation with Paul, Nalini smiled. "Interesting is definitely one word that I would use to describe Paul. I think he kind of had a crush on me, until he realized I wasn't into guys."

"I'm just not sure about him. I mean, it's not instant sparks like you and Lauren, with your tongues hanging out every time you see each other. You're obviously really into each other."

Nalini's cheeks flushed. "Is that how it seems to you?"

"You'd have to be blind not to notice." Emi snorted and attacked her plate, pulling it closer to her and away from Nalini's reach. "You two seem like you're the real deal."

"Hold on. We're just friends. I'm not really looking for a relationship. Anyway, we were talking about you and Paul, not me. Are you going to ask him out, or do I have to do that for you?"

"I don't need your help, thanks. It's just...well, it's been a while. My last relationship didn't end too well."

Nalini had never discussed Emi's past boyfriends, but she could sympathize with her reluctance to jump into a relationship. "Just have lunch or coffee with Paul, then. See how it goes. You don't need to rush into anything."

Emi grinned. "Maybe we can double-date sometime. That is, if you're dating Lauren. Where do things really stand with you two?"

"It's...complicated."

* * *

"It's...complicated." Lauren dropped her backpack on the floor, straightened up, and noticed Josh's raised eyebrows. Memories of the party, and what followed, were still fresh in her mind. She glared at Josh, who simply responded with a smirk. "What? It just is."

He spread his hands. "It's okay if you don't want to tell me."

She heaved a sigh and slumped into the ugly suede armchair across from him. The texture of the worn fabric against her skin reminded her of the days when that chair was new. She used to come home from school with Josh, and they'd both jump into it, fighting for position. It was one of the few pieces of furniture he'd retained after his parents had sold the house and moved to Bangor for his father's job. He'd never admit it, but Lauren suspected Josh secretly agreed that it was an eyesore—an eighties piece of trash that, nevertheless, held so many memories.

There were times when she envied Josh's cozy, one-bedroom apartment. It occupied the upper level of a Cape Cod on Merrimac Lane, just off Route 22. The house had once belonged to an insurance agent, with the lower level being his office. He had sold it several years ago after retiring, and the current owner had converted it into two apartments. Lauren had only met Zhang Wei, the graduate student who lived below Josh, on one occasion. Josh rarely mentioned his roommate, because he was hardly ever around. It was almost as good as having an entire house to himself.

Although Lauren dreamed of having her own place, she had carefully avoided the subject ever since she'd moved back to Zachary. At first, she'd been uneasy about the prospect of leaving her mother alone. After Luke's death, her mother had struggled with depression, and it soon became clear to Lauren that she was not returning to college. She had also started drinking more, and it was only with Lauren's help that she'd finally managed to quit. As time went by and her mother's situation improved, the financial benefits of living at home were not lost on Lauren. Still, she looked forward to moving out of the house. Some day, she'd make that happen.

Josh stood up and stretched. "Would it help if I told you about my girl problems?"

Lauren looked up. "Since when did you start seeing someone?"

"I haven't, ever since you broke my heart."

"Idiot." She stuck her tongue out at him, feeling only slightly ridiculous.

"Well, I figured I could make up a convincing story, if it came to that. Look, this thing with Nalini, whatever it is, is obviously bothering you. I want to help if I can."

"I could talk about it, once I figure it out myself." Lauren took the soda he offered her, snapped the tab, and took a sip. The chilled, fizzy liquid seemed to soothe her nerves as it slid down her throat. "Now, tell me about the band. It seems like it's been ages since we've actually had time to catch up. We still have a month before the book signing, but there's always some little detail that I have to take care of. By the way, you have to make it to the signing, or I'll never forgive you. You could pretend you have a crush on Alyssa Forester, if that helps."

Josh grinned. "I have the date on my calendar already, and I'll make sure my shift at the garage is scheduled around it."

"Good. Jen's getting really excited." She stifled a yawn and stretched her legs out. "I guess I should be, too..."

"But?"

"I'm not sure. I guess I'm not very enthusiastic about anything today."

"Well, maybe I can cheer you up just a little." Josh leaned forward. "You did ask about the band, after all. We've been talking it over, and we decided to put together a demo playlist of original music. Kevin has a friend who knows someone at an indie label. It's a long shot, but we'll see if we can get him interested."

Lauren jumped up from her chair and embraced him. "Josh— that's wonderful!" She knew he'd been writing new songs for the past few months, although the band had locked themselves into a pattern of doing covers whenever she'd heard them play. She was far from an expert on music, but Lauren knew how much Josh enjoyed performing his own songs, and she thought the ones he'd shared with her were really good. He just needed a little more confidence in himself.

Josh disentangled himself from her embrace, grinning. "I figured you might like the idea." He placed a hand on Lauren's knee. "So now that I'm hot in pursuit of my dream, what are you going to do about yours?"

"I don't know anymore." To her surprise, Lauren realized she hadn't given the idea much thought for several weeks. Nalini was clearly having an influence on her life in more ways than one. "I mean, I still think I want to finish college, but it's just not going to happen right now."

"And why's that? It's not like you to give up that easily."

Clearly, Josh wasn't going to let this go. He could be infuriatingly persistent at times. Lauren shot him a glare, but it had no effect.

"Okay, I'll make you a deal. If you get that recording contract, I'll fill out my application for the next semester."

He frowned. "Not good enough. You have to submit it, too."

Lauren threw up her hands. "Fine. After I complete the application, you can make sure I send it in. Deal?"

He shook her hand. "Deal."

SEVENTEEN

I N A WAY, Lauren was grateful that preparations for the book signing had consumed so much of her time over the past few days. Although she and Nalini had texted occasionally, there had been little opportunity to meet, and neither one of them appeared willing to make the first move. Lauren hated to admit it but, in her case, she was simply avoiding the issue. Nalini had promised to be there for the big event, though.

The night before, Jen had introduced Lauren to Alyssa Forester over dinner. The author had turned out to be vivacious and approachable, with a great sense of humor. Lauren could see why Jen and Alyssa got along so well. If Lauren hadn't known better, she'd have assumed they were family.

Now, with less than an hour to go before the store opened, Lauren was catching some of Jen's excitement. And, of course, there was the prospect of seeing Nalini again.

"There are people lining up already," Jen said, carrying an armful of books. "I don't remember people lining up for anything, except during the Harry Potter days. That was long before you started working here." She walked to the table set up near the store entrance and arranged the books in neat piles, then stepped back to adjust the floor-standing banner that displayed a giant cover image of Alyssa's latest book.

"Well, it's not often that you get celebrities signing books here." Lauren moved a box of books underneath the table. Jen had told her to keep a backup stash handy, in case they'd underestimated the demand. Since Alyssa was self-published, the store simply sold her books on consignment, taking their customary forty percent cut, and Alyssa provided the stock. Anything left over after the signing would go in a prime spot on the store's shelves, but Lauren expected they wouldn't sit there for very long, if Alyssa's track record to date was any indication.

A short while later, Alyssa arrived, using the back entrance as Jen requested. She looked dazzling, wearing a white silk blouson top and blue jeans that looked brand new, unlike Lauren's faded pair with a few rips that had nothing to do with fashion. Alyssa greeted Jen with a hug and smiled at Lauren. Chelsea, who had agreed to put in an extra shift, was busy in the back but came running out when she heard Alyssa was in the store.

"I'm such a big fan," Chelsea said, almost tripping over her own feet. "I've read all your books, Ms. Forester."

Lauren bit back a giggle. She knew Chelsea devoured romance novels, but she had never expected Chelsea to go gaga over an author like this. Alyssa took it all in stride, thanking Chelsea for being a devoted fan, and offering to make Chelsea a member of her "street team." It was no small honor. Lauren was acutely aware of how important a street team was to an independent author. What better way to spread the word of a new release than to have a legion of fans sing its praises on social media?

When opening time finally arrived, Lauren and Chelsea took their spots at the counter and double-checked that the iPads running the store's point-of-sale software were functioning. Lauren remembered the last occasion when their Internet service was down during a busy period, and they'd had to ask customers to pay with cash or make arrangements to invoice the buyers later. Jen had reminisced about the days of processing credit cards with carbon copies and something she affectionately called a "knuckle buster." Lauren had heard of this mythical machine, but she'd never actually seen one.

With a wave at Alyssa, Jen opened the doors. The group of people waiting outside filed in, forming a line in front of the book-signing table. Lauren watched as Alyssa chatted with the first customer, picked up a book from the pile at her elbow, and signed it. The woman reacted much as Chelsea had, apparently unable to believe she was in the presence of the famous author at last.

Once again, Lauren wondered if her own feeble attempts at writing would ever get her to the point where readers would be lining up to see her. With a sigh, she decided it was better not to focus on those thoughts. What hope could someone without a college degree have? Despite the deal she'd made with Josh, Lauren remained uncertain about her future. She forced a smile as she served the next customer, who had apparently rummaged through the shelves and purchased every book in Alyssa's current series, in addition to the new release she'd signed.

After the initial rush subsided, Lauren was able to catch her breath. She kept checking the door, hoping to see Nalini walk through it. The book signing was scheduled to end at noon, and she was sure that Nalini had said she'd stop by, even though she'd never read any of Alyssa's books. True to his word, Josh had visited the bookstore earlier, but he hadn't stayed long.

"Looks like we have a few customers who aren't looking for romance novels." Jen paused at the counter and glanced back at the stacks. "Lauren, go ahead and see if they need any help. Chelsea and I can handle things here."

Grateful for a distraction, Lauren made her way down the narrow aisles. She had perfected the art of hovering just within range of a customer—not intruding on their browsing, but being close enough to help if they had a question.

After directing a couple of students to the science fiction shelves, she busied herself with cleaning up some of the books, straightening the rows and moving a few that had fallen out of order.

"Lauren?" A hand rested gently on her shoulder, and Lauren's heartbeat sped up. Nalini had made it, after all.

She spun around and dropped the books she was holding. "Oh my god. Kelly!"

"I...um...I heard about the signing, and I thought I'd make the trip over here. It's good to see you." Kelly twisted a strand of her hair around one finger.

Lauren's gut churned, and she struggled to stem the onslaught of memories that came rushing back. The cold anger that she'd felt about Kelly's betrayal had, in time, been replaced with a dull numbness, but one look into those expressive hazel eyes could still awaken a flicker of desire in her. She exhaled slowly and tried to avoid letting her gaze linger on Kelly's lips.

"How have you been?"

Kelly bit her lower lip. "Can't complain. Look, can we get lunch or something once the signing is over? I'd really like to catch up with you before I head back to Portland tomorrow night."

Every instinct told Lauren this was a bad idea, but she nodded. After all, it was just one lunch, and it wasn't like Kelly was moving back to Zachary or anything. Besides, it didn't look like Nalini was going to show up, after all, and Lauren's heart was heavy with disappointment. "I'll see if I can get a longer lunch break."

"Great!" Kelly took Lauren's hand and squeezed it, sending an electric pulse up Lauren's arm. "I'll stop back here around noon."

After Kelly had left, Lauren remained in the stacks for a while, trying to process what had just happened. Of all people, she hadn't expected to see Kelly at the signing. Unless things had changed after they broke up, Kelly didn't even read that much, let alone read straight romances, so she'd obviously come to the bookstore just to see Lauren.

Jen was perfectly understanding about Lauren needing to take a longer lunch, but Lauren was careful not to mention whom she was meeting. Jen had been furious with Kelly when she'd found out about the breakup, and Lauren was sure Jen's opinion of Kelly hadn't changed much. She still couldn't help wondering what had brought Kelly back to town. They hadn't kept in touch after Kelly had moved away, and Lauren had no desire to start now.

The crowd of ardent Alyssa Forester fans thinned out as it got past eleven, although Lauren suspected they'd probably run over the officially advertised time. Every time the doorbell rang, Lauren looked up to see if it was Nalini. Finally, with a just a few minutes left, she gave up watching the door.

After all, what did it matter if Nalini missed the signing? It wasn't like she was interested in Alyssa's books anyway. Still, it would have been nice to see her. The memory of their last night together, despite being almost a month ago, still sent Lauren's stomach into a weird flip. Nalini's hands running through Lauren's hair, her fingers gently probing between Lauren's thighs...

"Earth to Lauren. Hello?"

Lauren jerked back to reality. "Sorry, Chelsea. What were you saying?"

Chelsea chuckled. "You were really on another planet. I just said that I know it's just an hour to lunch, but if you need to take lunch early, I can cover for you."

"Thanks." Lauren didn't really need a break yet but was grateful for the option. She checked her phone. "I could use some fresh air. I'm just going to step outside for a few."

"Take your time." Chelsea waved a hand, displaying elegantly manicured nails, each of which was painted a different color of the rainbow.

Lauren headed for the door, stepped outside, and took a deep breath. She leaned against the storefront and closed her eyes for a moment, trying to slow down her heart rate.

"Sorry I'm late. I thought I'd never get here. My mother called, and..."

With a gasp, Lauren opened her eyes and blinked. Nalini was standing right in front of her, close enough to kiss, a quizzical smile turning up the corners of her mouth.

"I'm glad you came." Lauren's pulse began to quicken again. She swallowed hard. "Would you like to meet Alyssa?"

"Actually, I came to ask if you wanted to grab lunch. I know we haven't had much of a chance to talk since the last time we...well...for the past few weeks. My schedule just keeps getting crazier, with all the research assignments for my classes."

Lauren's heart sank. Why did Kelly have to come back into her life, especially now? "I, um...I'd love to, but I can't. I already have plans." She hoped Kelly wouldn't show up early for lunch. Introducing her to Nalini would feel more awkward than it should.

Nalini raised her eyebrows but, to Lauren's relief, she didn't press the issue. "Okay. Maybe we can catch up tonight, then. I'll text you later."

When Lauren went back inside, there were just a handful of people waiting at the table. Lauren tried to imagine what it must feel like to be Alyssa Forester. From everything Lauren had heard, Alyssa worked a grueling schedule, publishing a new book every month. But then, she probably enjoyed what she did.

"Being an indie author is as much about marketing as it is writing," Alyssa had said earlier that day. "Yes, writing is important. But if you can't sell books, the best writing in the world won't help you."

One day, Lauren hoped she'd be doing her own book signing.

EIGHTEEN

"THIS PLACE HASN'T changed one bit." Kelly looked around the room and grinned at Tony, who was helping another customer. He glanced at her, and his eyes widened.

Lauren smirked. "It's not like you've been gone that long, Kelly." Some things never changed. As usual, Kelly had asked Lauren to order for her, and Lauren knew exactly what Kelly liked on her personal-sized pizza: sausage, ham, pepperoni, and extra cheese. Her only concession to the plant kingdom was black olives.

Kelly turned her full attention to Lauren. "Does that mean you missed me?"

"Are we really having this conversation?" Lauren couldn't help the surge of anger that constricted her throat. She'd tried to give Kelly the benefit of the doubt when she'd agreed to meet for lunch, but it was hard to let the past stay buried. And yet, watching the light play on the strands of Kelly's dark hair, following the curve of her cheek, and noticing that she still used the same, barely perceptible shade of lip gloss had awakened old emotions within Lauren. Predominant among these was a hunger she would rather have not acknowledged.

"Sorry." Kelly threw up her hands. "I'll behave, I promise." She winked and walked her fingers across the table toward Lauren's hand. "Unless you'd like me not to?"

"Just...why did you come back here?" Lauren took a deep breath, but her nerves were still jangling.

Fortunately, Tony arrived at that moment with their salads. "It's good to see you again, Kelly. You ladies let me know if you need anything else, okay?"

"Thanks, Tony." Kelly gave him her most charming smile. "It's good to be back, although I'm not here for long."

After Tony had left, Lauren waited while Kelly fussed with her salad. She wasn't going to let Kelly off the hook on this one.

Kelly finally looked up, and Lauren raised her eyebrows. "So? Why did you show up for the book signing? I'm pretty sure you haven't suddenly become a huge Alyssa Forester fan."

"God, no." Kelly put down her fork. "I came to see you, actually. And...well, first of all, to apologize about how we ended things between us."

"You cheated on me. That's how we ended things. You're apologizing...now?" Lauren's chest constricted from the pain of her vivid memories. The day she finally confronted Kelly. The hot tears running down her face as Kelly admitted she'd slept with Sydney, a student at the university. The anger that Lauren had felt welling up inside her finally bursting through, like a dam being breached. Lauren walking out of Kelly's apartment, knowing she'd never set foot in it again.

"I know what this sounds like. I should have realized how much I'd hurt you." She took Lauren's hands and, this time, Lauren didn't pull away. "I'm really sorry, Lauren. Maybe being away for almost a year has made me realize exactly how sorry I am. Can you ever forgive me?"

Lauren took a deep breath. Of all the reasons for Kelly's return to Zachary, she hadn't expected this. "I don't know if I can right now. Maybe, in time, I will."

Kelly's bottom lip quivered, and she squeezed Lauren's hand. "I hope you can. I'm thinking about moving back here permanently."

It was as if someone had suddenly pulled the chair out from under Lauren. She clutched at the edge of the table, struggling to breathe. "Why?" It was the only word she could manage.

"I miss my family. Sure, I get to see them on holidays, but that's not enough. Also, my job in Portland isn't that great, and I actually miss living in a small town, much to my surprise. I'm sure I can find some work here." She leaned forward, and Lauren forced herself to tear her gaze away from Kelly's plump lips. "Most of all, I miss you. I want us to start over, Lauren. I want things to be the way they were before."

Before you cheated on me. The words were on the tip of Lauren's tongue, but she didn't utter them. "I don't think that's a good idea."

Kelly's eyes narrowed. "Are you seeing someone?"

"Yes. No. I don't know. Anyway, it doesn't matter. That's not the point." Why was Kelly making her so flustered? Lauren had always been the calm, rational one in their relationship. Deciding to move back to Zachary on a whim was exactly something that Kelly would do.

"You don't know if you're seeing someone?" Kelly's perfectly sculpted eyebrows shot up.

"Let it go, Kelly. If you're thinking about moving back solely on my account, please don't." And yet...Lauren couldn't entirely dismiss the idea, now that Kelly had planted the seed in her head. What did she really have with Nalini? They were friends with benefits, just as they'd reassured each other. There wasn't anything deeper than that. No prospects for a long-term relationship, based on what Nalini had said.

Were there?

* * *

Since Nalini had got a ride into town with Emi and suddenly found herself without lunch plans, she considered checking if they could meet up. However, the unexpected disappointment she'd felt after leaving the bookstore convinced her that the fifteen-minute walk back to campus would do her some good.

Why was she so upset about a little thing like Lauren being unavailable for lunch? It wasn't like they had made definite plans, and Nalini had known Lauren would be busy with the book signing. As she turned onto River Street and headed toward Route 1, Nalini glanced over her shoulder, as if expecting to catch a glimpse of Lauren following her. She shook her head.

Nalini inhaled sharply as she stepped onto the bridge. Thanks to Lauren, she'd now learned that the pedestrian walkway across the river was part of a recent project to widen Route 1 as it crossed the Zachary River. Although she'd done this a few times now, she still gripped the handrail for a moment and then took several deep breaths before proceeding.

Quickening her pace, Nalini resolved to call Lauren later that day. For now, she focused on getting to the end of the bridge. She heaved a sigh as she finally stepped off it and took the road that led back to campus.

Now that she was breathing normally again, more pleasant thoughts came to Nalini's mind—glimpses of Lauren in her bed the last time they'd made love. She licked her lips as she remembered how good Lauren's tongue had felt teasing her nipples, and how they'd responded immediately, sending waves of pleasure through her body. Most of all, Nalini had enjoyed the simple intimacy of lying in bed next to Lauren, despite their cramped surroundings. Telling Lauren about the situation with parents had been difficult, but Nalini was glad she'd done it, even though it still hurt to know that her relationship with Lauren could never lead to anything more. Nalini had convinced herself that what they had right now was all she could expect.

Her phone pinged with a text message. *You still in town? Need a ride home?*

She smiled. It was just like Emi to check up on her. She thumbed a reply. *No, thanks. I walked back.*

Just as Nalini was about to close the app, another text came through. Lauren's photo popped up on the screen, and Nalini's heart beat just a little faster.

Sorry about lunch. Can we talk tonight?

Nalini started typing a reply, reassuring Lauren that it was okay and that she would love to see Lauren, but she deleted it and went with a single-word response instead: *Sure.*

Great! OK if I stop by your dorm around 8?

Of course. See you then.

Nalini returned to her dorm with a spring in her step. A while later, a knock on the door startled her, making her drop the book she'd been reading. She must have fallen asleep. She checked her phone and frowned. It was a little after five, too early for Lauren.

Another knock sounded. "Nalini? Are you there? It's Emi."

Nalini jumped up and opened the door. "Sorry. I must have dozed off. Come on in."

Emi glanced at the book on the floor and chuckled. "It must not have been a very interesting book, then." She settled into the solitary armchair that sat in a corner of the room. "So, how did your lunch with Lauren go?"

"It didn't." Nalini shrugged. "She couldn't make it, but she's meeting me tonight."

"Is everything okay with you two?"

"We're fine. I told you before. We're just friends."

"Are you sure?" Emi cocked her head.

With a sigh, Nalini plopped down on the bed. "Just because Lauren and I had sex doesn't mean we're in a serious relationship, Emi."

"I guess I still don't quite get that. I mean, I've only had two boyfriends, so maybe it's different for me. Of course, neither relationship lasted that long, but I really did feel something with both of them."

"Speaking of boyfriends..." Nalini seized the opportunity to change the subject. "How are things going with Paul? I couldn't help noticing that you two have been spending more time together lately."

"Well, he's definitely interesting. I still feel like I don't know a lot about him, but I can't quite explain why I'm attracted to him."

Nalini grinned. "Maybe you two were meant to be together. After all, when two brilliant scientists meet, there's bound to be some...biochemistry. Even if one of them is a physicist."

Emi groaned and glared at Nalini. "At times, I don't think Paul is even aware I exist."

"Oh, he knows you exist. Trust me."

Emi's expression brightened. "Why? Has he been asking about me?"

Nalini wasn't entirely sure if she relished the role of matchmaker. "Paul is certainly interesting. I'll give you that. When I first met him, I thought he just came on to every woman he met, but it turned out that he's actually pretty reserved—even shy—and that was his way of compensating. Or rather, overcompensating."

Emi hauled herself out of the armchair. "Maybe I'll go see if he's in his room. It's almost time for dinner."

"You do that." Nalini escorted Emi to the door and squeezed her shoulder. "Just don't get him started on D-branes and p-branes."

Emi giggled. "Thanks for the tip."

After Emi had left, Nalini decided to eat an early dinner as well, except hers was at the Union cafeteria, sitting alone at a table in the back. She planned to be back in her dorm room well before it was time for Lauren to show up. She picked up her book again but soon set it aside, finding it difficult to focus on the intricacies of Vikram Chandra's rich narrative.

When Lauren arrived a few minutes after eight, Nalini pulled her inside and kissed her with a hunger that surprised them both. Although Lauren responded at first, something wasn't quite right. Nalini released her and held her at arm's length, searching her captivating blue eyes for a hint.

"What's wrong?" She led Lauren to the bed and sat down beside her.

Lauren's lower lip trembled. "I met Kelly today. That's why I couldn't have lunch with you."

Nalini's chest tightened, and she swallowed hard. "Kelly, as in your ex?"

"She came to the signing. Well, as it turned out, she wasn't really here to meet Alyssa Forester." Lauren sucked in a deep breath. "She...she wanted to get back together."

"Did you say yes?"

"What? No, of course not." Lauren turned to face Nalini. "How could I?"

Nalini took Lauren's hand. A sudden chill made her shiver, despite her always overheated dorm room. "It's okay, Lauren. I'm sure you must still have some feelings for her. If you want to get back together with Kelly, I totally understand."

"I don't want Kelly." Lauren seized Nalini's face with both hands and kissed her. "I want you. Even if this...what we have now...isn't going to be forever. I know that now, and I hate that we can't be anything more, but I want to enjoy every minute of the time we have together, while we still have it."

A tear trickled down Nalini's cheek. "I want that, too." The hollow ache inside her, knowing how much she wanted their relationship to be so much more, only seemed to grow with the jolt of pleasure from Lauren's kiss.

Lauren brushed her thumb across Nalini's cheek. "There's something else I wanted to ask you. Do you have plans for Thanksgiving?"

"Not really. Normally, I'd be in Boston with my aunt and uncle, but I haven't talked to them about it this year."

"Well, now you do. Spend it with us. My mom would love to have you."

Nalini smiled and nodded. "What about you? How do you feel about having me?"

Lauren's kiss was all the response Nalini needed.

NINETEEN

URING NALINI'S YEARS at Wellesley, the week leading up to Thanksgiving had been a time of anticipation. She had always looked forward to spending the holiday with her aunt and uncle in Boston. They were the closest family she had in America, and the appeal of a family gathering for the holiday reminded her of similar traditions growing up in India.

This year was different, in more ways than one. Ever since a fateful call from her parents a few days earlier, Nalini had been dreading every moment that brought her closer to facing her destiny. Her parents had booked her airline tickets for a trip home during the Christmas break. This was no ordinary vacation, though. Her worst fears had been realized. They'd told her, in no uncertain terms, that if she wanted their continuing financial support, she would need to finalize wedding arrangements during her stay in Mumbai. The astrologers had already picked two auspicious wedding dates, and her future husband's family was eager to meet her.

After crying into her pillow for several minutes, Nalini had called her aunt and uncle. They'd been sympathetic and had promised to talk to her parents, but Nalini knew nothing would change the outcome. Nalini had said nothing to Lauren, but she'd been steeling herself to discuss it over Thanksgiving. Spending the day with Lauren would be a solitary ray of light to pierce the cloud of despair that had been hanging over her head.

Now, as she struggled to find a comfortable spot in bed, she tried to set everything else aside. Tomorrow, she'd be seeing Lauren again. The surge of pleasure that the thought evoked was tempered with sadness this time. What would things be like between them a year from now, next Thanksgiving? Would Lauren even want to see her after she was married?

She buried her face in the pillow, wanting to scream with frustration. How was she ever going to live with Nikhil, a man she knew only from photographs? The only consolation was that he wouldn't expect her to quit school and move back to India, a fate that had befallen one of her former classmates. Nikhil's brother was a US citizen, and Nikhil had already applied for a green card. Nalini would have a year or two of freedom, married but separated from her husband geographically, before she truly had to deal with the realities of marital life. She shuddered to think about having sex with a man. Would she be able to smile and fake it, as her aunt had advised during their candid conversation?

Nalini sighed. It was no use speculating about a future that still seemed unreal. She'd have to tell Lauren everything and hope that, at the very least, they could still remain friends.

Waking up in darkness didn't help Nalini's mood much. It was one aspect of winter in downeast Maine that she hated, made worse by the nonsensical ritual of ending Daylight Saving Time. By the time she made it to the kitchenette for a light breakfast, however, her spirits had lifted just a little. She popped a couple of frozen waffles into the toaster and made a passably decent cup of coffee from the single-serve machine that had been installed recently. It wasn't as good as the coffee from the cafeteria, of course, but since just about everything on campus was closed, her options this morning were limited.

She spent the next few hours catching up with e-mail and watching music videos on her phone. Lauren had insisted on picking Nalini up at Jorgensen Hall and Nalini, grateful for a reprieve from having to walk across the river in freezing weather, hadn't protested too much. She almost dropped her phone when Lauren's text came through. She picked up her backpack, smiling at the memory of Lauren's suggestion that she spend the night. After a quick glance at the mirror, she took a deep breath, tucked a strand of hair behind her ear, and headed for the door.

Lauren greeted her with a huge grin. Then, after Nalini had buckled herself in, Lauren leaned in for a kiss that left Nalini yearning for more. A lot more. She pinned her arms against her stomach. Would Lauren still want to kiss her after she broke the news?

"Mom's really looking forward to this," Lauren said. "It's usually just the two of us for Thanksgiving."

"I'm so glad you invited me." Nalini placed a hand on Lauren's thigh as the car moved forward.

"Were your aunt and uncle really disappointed you wouldn't be with them for the holidays?"

"They were, at first." Nalini squeezed Lauren's thigh, unable to control her impulses. "I explained where I was going to be, though, and they came around. They even told me I should bring you to Boston some time."

"So, they know about us? I mean, whatever 'us' is."

"They're fairly progressive, actually, given how the rest of my family views the world." Nalini chuckled, trying to cover her unease at Lauren's question. "My uncle is the complete opposite of my dad. He met my aunt when they were both graduate students at Boston University. They fell in love and got married a year later." She squinted at Lauren, realizing she hadn't addressed Lauren's question. "They know we're having sex, if that's what you mean."

Lauren stared at the road ahead. "So not all Hindu marriages are arranged?"

"No. It depends on the family." Nalini shifted in her seat. The conversation was heading in a direction she wasn't prepared to discuss yet. On the one hand, this would be a good opportunity to get everything off her chest. On the other—selfishly, if she was being honest—she didn't want to ruin the day with Lauren already. "Of course, my uncle and aunt have spent more than half their lives in this country now, so things are quite different for them. I was born after my uncle had left India, so I only saw him every few years when he came back to visit. We used to talk a lot on the phone, though. I know it sounds weird but, in some ways, I feel closer to him than my dad."

"I can understand that. I didn't really know much about my dad. He left when I was five years old."

"I'm sorry." Nalini's hand hovered near Lauren's thigh again, but she pulled it back. Lauren's attention remained focused on the road. "I didn't know that. I can't imagine what that must be like."

"It's not so bad. I think mom tried to keep in touch after they got divorced. She kept asking him to come visit once in a while, but he never did." Lauren exhaled slowly. "I'd like to give him the benefit of the doubt and think that seeing us might stir up painful memories or something. However, from what mom's told me, I don't think that's the case."

"I grew up with large family gatherings that were held at every possible occasion." Nalini smiled, wrapped in memories like a warm blanket. "Birthdays, anniversaries, religious holidays, even celebrating good grades at school—there was always an excuse to have a party."

Lauren turned her head, and their eyes met for a moment. "Do you miss it?"

"I did when I arrived in Boston, although at least I had my aunt and uncle. Parties here are pretty different. The ones I remember from my childhood were more about spending time with family and stuffing ourselves with plenty of good food." She laughed as she thought back to the party she'd dragged Lauren to a couple of months earlier. It seemed like years ago now.

"After I'd lived here for a while, though, I got used to not having family around all the time."

They exited the bridge, and Lauren turned onto River Street. As the now-familiar Cape Cod with lemon-cream siding and a distinctive, brick-red front door came into view, Nalini suddenly realized she was arriving empty-handed.

"Crap! Lauren, I'm so sorry. I didn't bring anything."

"No worries." Lauren pulled into the driveway and turned off the engine. "We didn't expect you to, and mom pretty much has everything covered. She's even doing a Tofurkey roast, along with the turkey."

Nalini got out of her seat and immediately pulled Lauren in for a hug. "This is going to be a wonderful Thanksgiving. I really am glad to be here."

Lauren's lips were warm on hers, and Nalini sighed deeply as she tasted a hint of strawberry. "I'm glad you're here, too."

When Nalini stepped inside, Michelle welcomed her with a hug. Nalini's offer to help with cooking was declined at once, and Lauren urged her to make herself comfortable in the living room. She settled into a spot on the couch, feeling a bit awkward by herself while Lauren and Michelle worked in the kitchen, but Lauren soon came out to join her.

"This feels good," Lauren said, resting her head on Nalini's shoulder. "We're almost done in the kitchen. Can I get you something to drink?"

Nalini accepted a glass of hot spiced cider. "Lauren, are you sure you don't need my help?"

"Positive." Lauren gave Nalini a quick kiss. "If it makes you feel better, you can help with the dishes after we're done eating, and we're all too stuffed to move a muscle. How's that sound?"

"Deal." Nalini put her arm around Lauren's shoulder and pulled her closer. "Do I get to kiss the cook?"

"Well, I don't know. I'll have to ask mom how she feels about that."

"Didn't you cook, too?"

Lauren grinned. "I did help with the food prep, but mom did most of it, really. She always does. It's her thing. She loves the holidays."

The meal was everything Nalini had envisioned and more. The Tofurkey roast was set in front of her, while Lauren carved the turkey. All the traditional favorites adorned the table: creamy mashed potatoes and home-made gravy, stuffing, green bean casserole, sweet potatoes, and Michelle's special cranberry sauce that made Nalini moan with pleasure when she tasted it, earning her a sly look from Lauren. Best of all, she felt right at home with the two of them. The only thing that marred the meal was her fear that she might never have the opportunity to share a holiday meal with them again.

After several helpings of everything except the turkey, Nalini could barely summon enough energy to get out of her chair. She managed to help Lauren collect up the dishes, rinse them, and place them in the dishwasher. Lauren insisted that Michelle should rest up while she and Nalini put the leftovers away.

Nalini couldn't help admiring Lauren's perfect ass, showcased by her skinny jeans, while she bent over to move a few dishes on the bottom shelf of the refrigerator. She was looking forward to spending the night with Lauren, but she'd also braced herself for the possibility that nothing might happen between them after she'd told Lauren about the trip home for Christmas. She knew she had to do it soon—rip off the band-aid and face the consequences—but a part of her wished she could postpone the inevitable for just a few days longer.

TWENTY

LAUREN SETTLED DOWN next to Nalini on the couch. This felt good. At the moment, she wanted nothing more than to feel the heat of Nalini's body pressed against her own, curl up, and take a nap. She'd been looking forward to Thanksgiving all week.

The three of them were in a post-Thanksgiving meal stupor, gathered around the TV. Lauren's mother flipped through the channels and glanced at Nalini.

"Are you a football fan, Nalini?"

"Not really." Nalini turned to face her "I mean, I've watched a few Patriots games with some of my friends at Wellesley, but football never really appealed to me. I'm more of a baseball person, actually." She stifled a yawn and giggled when Lauren immediately did the same. "Of course, I grew up with cricket, which is something most Americans don't understand at all, but baseball is my second favorite sport now. My uncle took me to a game at Fenway, and I fell in love with the park."

"I can understand that." Lauren's mother smiled and handed the remote control to Lauren as she stood up. "I do like baseball, but watching it on TV isn't the same thing as being at the game. We have a family tradition of watching old movies on Thanksgiving, if that's more up your alley."

"That sounds perfect." Nalini put an arm around Lauren and pulled her closer. Lauren sighed with contentment as she brought up her streaming queue, and she gave Nalini the first pick.

"*Witness for the Prosecution*? I don't think I've seen that one." Her mother returned from the kitchen with a fresh pitcher of warm spiced cider and refilled Nalini's glass.

Nalini's face lit up. "I think you'll enjoy it. I barely remember it now, but it made a huge impact as a kid. Marlene Dietrich was magnificent, from what I recall."

Although Lauren's turkey-induced drowsiness threatened to overcome her at first, she soon got into the movie, and her lethargy faded. It also helped that the delicious sensations evoked by Nalini's warmth, and the thrill of Nalini's fingers absently running through Lauren's hair, were combining to spark a fire deep within her. She'd been both surprised and pleased when Nalini had accepted her invitation to spend the night. It had been a while since the last time they'd had sex. Over a month, according to her calculations. A shiver ran through her as she pictured Nalini's naked body writhing under hers, and she snuggled closer.

Lauren stole a glance at Nalini, who appeared to be engrossed in the movie. Something seemed different. Although Nalini hadn't pulled away physically, Lauren got the sense that an invisible barrier had formed between them somehow. Was it something she'd said or done? She frowned, distracted from the black and white images on the screen for a moment as she replayed the day in her head. She'd have to talk to Nalini about it as soon as they had some privacy. Whatever it was, she hoped there'd be a simple explanation and that they could straighten out the issue. Despite her firm resolve not to, over the past week Lauren had realized she was falling for Nalini. It was a silly thing to do, and ultimately futile, so she'd convinced herself she wouldn't say anything to Nalini.

After the movie ended, it was her mother's turn to pick. Lauren was not at all surprised when they ended up watching an old musical from the fifties. *The King and I* was one of her mother's favorites, but Lauren had never watched the entire movie. Once again, Nalini appeared to be enjoying the movie thoroughly, but Lauren still couldn't shake the sensation that something was wrong.

When they took a break, Lauren gave Nalini a quick kiss. "I'm looking forward to tonight," she whispered in Nalini's ear. "Mom made up the guest bedroom for you, but I doubt we'll need it."

Nalini avoided Lauren's gaze as they headed for the kitchen, although she managed a weak smile.

That wasn't the reaction Lauren had expected. She had to find out what was going on.

"Nalini, what's wrong?" She paused halfway through assembling a turkey sandwich. "Are you okay? Is it something I said?"

This time, Nalini looked directly into her eyes. "I'm fine. It's just...well, we have something to discuss."

"Can we talk now? Is it serious? Have you met someone else?" Lauren's imagination began to run wild. She took a deep breath, trying to regain control over her emotions.

Nalini gave her a hug. "Let's wait until after the movie. I'm fine. I promise."

Somehow, Lauren doubted the sincerity of that promise, but she shrugged and let it go. After they returned to the living room, she settled back onto the couch next to Nalini again. Although their bodies still touched, the distance between them might well have been as wide as the Grand Canyon.

When the credits finally started rolling, Lauren's mother stood up and yawned. "Unfortunately, I have to work the early shift tomorrow, so I'd better get to bed. You two keep watching, though. I believe it's Lauren's turn to pick something."

"I think I'm all moved out for tonight, mom." Lauren stared at Nalini. "Maybe we should call it a night, too."

Her mother smiled. "Planning on an early start tomorrow, too? I'm sure you two could snag some good deals at the Black Friday sales."

Nalini shook her head. "I don't think anything would entice me to get out of bed before five in the morning."

"Well, good night, then. I'll try not to wake you when I leave for work. This really was a wonderful Thanksgiving." Lauren's mother hugged them both before heading off to her bedroom.

Lauren grabbed Nalini's hand, led her to the bedroom, and sat down on the edge of her bed. "Okay, you have to tell me what's going on. I've been trying to figure out what I've done to upset you, and it's driving me crazy."

Nalini sat down beside Lauren and sighed. "You haven't done anything." She took Lauren's hands in hers. "I wanted to discuss it with you earlier, but I just couldn't do it." She swallowed hard. "I guess we both knew this day would come, but I didn't think it would happen this soon." With a visible effort, her eyes met Lauren's.

Lauren listened without saying a word, her heart sinking as Nalini poured out her story. She was going back to India over the Christmas break so her parents could finalize her arranged marriage. Lauren's worst fears had come true. Her initial shock turned to something else, cold and hard as steel, as she processed what this meant for them. She had already come to terms with her own feelings for Nalini, and the only bright spot in all of this was that she hadn't made a fool of herself by saying anything. Once again, a woman she loved had hurt her beyond measure.

She fought an impulse to brush away the tears away from Nalini's eyes with her fingers. "So...this is it, then? You're planning to go through with it?" Lauren's voice trembled, but she managed to keep her own tears away.

Nalini's entire body shook with her sobs. Her pain was evident, but Lauren had grown numb in order to protect her own heart. It was the only defense she knew. Finally, Nalini looked up at Lauren again.

"I...I have to. I don't have a choice."

"You always have a choice, Nalini." Lauren's voice broke, and her tears finally came. When Nalini reached for her, she turned away.

Neither of them spoke for a while. Lauren slowly regained some of her composure, and the day seemed to catch up with her all at once. She fought the wave of exhaustion that seemed certain to engulf her.

"Lauren...I can leave now, if you want to be alone. I can walk back."

The pleading note in Nalini's voice pierced the barrier between them. She shook her head. "It's late. I still want you to stay. But I think it's best if you use the guest bedroom, after all."

After she had made sure Nalini was comfortable, Lauren returned to her bedroom and shut the door. Still dressed, she settled in under the covers but, despite her exhaustion, her brain refused to shut down.

The more she reflected on what had happened, the more she realized that she couldn't blame Nalini alone. After all, Nalini had been quite clear, from the outset, that a long-term relationship was never an option for them. For a while, Lauren had been content to enjoy what they had, while they still had it, hoping that the day of reckoning would never come.

Unfortunately, she'd made the mistake of falling in love with Nalini along the way. Lauren wondered if things would be different now, if she'd told Nalini how she felt. Clearly, Nalini didn't feel the same way about Lauren, because this ridiculous arranged marriage wouldn't be happening if she did.

Try as she might, Lauren still couldn't wrap her head around the idea. Marrying a stranger, especially one to whom you would never be attracted sexually, just didn't make any sense. She could sympathize with Nalini's predicament to some extent. Being financially dependent on her parents certainly complicated things. But surely they wouldn't disown their only daughter just for refusing to marry the man they'd picked out for her?

Lauren still remembered the day she'd come out to her mother. While her mother seemed surprised at the time by the news, she'd hugged Lauren and offered her support right away. Of course, Lauren knew not all parents were that supportive. She could only imagine how Nalini's parents would react, based on everything she'd heard about them.

Maybe she was just being selfish. She wanted...needed...Nalini in her life, and it was blinding her to the considerable challenges that Nalini was facing.

Could they still be friends, though, like Nalini wanted? Kelly's surprise visit at the book signing had reminded Lauren that their breakup still hurt, but time had dulled some of the pian. She could at least be civil to Kelly now, which was something that had seemed impossible right after they'd broken up.

For the moment, what she needed was some distance from Nalini, so she could deal with her grief. Fortunately, in a few weeks, Nalini would be thousands of miles away. Meanwhile, Lauren would continue to keep that barrier around her heart. The alternative was just too painful to consider.

After managing to navigate a few awkward moments over breakfast the next morning, Lauren steeled herself for the short ride back to Nalini's dorm. She drove in silence, but when Nalini broke down in tears after they arrived, Lauren had to fight the instinct to take Nalini into her arms.

"Please, Lauren," Nalini whispered, dabbing at her eyes with her sleeve. "I really don't want to lose you as a friend. Can I at least call you sometime?"

"I'm really not sure that's a good idea." Lauren bit her lip. "I just...I need some time."

She watched Nalini enter the building, shoulders bent. The pain of separation sliced through her like a knife, and Lauren bowed her head. She clutched the wheel with both hands and finally gave in to the flood of emotion that threatened to drown her, hot tears running down her cheeks. It was a while before she was able to put the car into gear and drive away.

TWENTY-ONE

NALINI SURVEYED HER dorm room once more, then glanced at the travel list she'd compiled on her phone. She started checking off entries but was interrupted by a knock at the door.

"Hey, it's Emi!"

"Come on in. It's open."

Emi peeked around the door. "Looks like you're all packed. I just wanted to say goodbye before I left."

Nalini gave her a hug. "Thanks. I was just going over my travel list." She showed Emi her phone.

"I'm impressed. I'm leaving in a few hours, and I haven't even started packing. I'm not going halfway across the world, though."

With a sheepish grin, Nalini put her phone away. "My friends at Wellesley used to tease me about my obsession with lists. Honestly, I'm not that organized when it comes to most other things. Traveling freaks me out, though. I always try to pack my suitcase at least a day in advance. Even then, I keep dreading that I'll be at the airport when I remember I've left something critical behind."

"Yeah, I know what you mean." Emi sat down on the corner of the bed while Nalini zipped up her suitcase.

"That's the last of it. I just have to finish packing my carry-on bag tomorrow morning."

Emi looked her in the eye. "So, you're really going through with the whole arranged marriage thing?"

Nalini sat beside Emi and wrung her hands. "I don't have much of a choice. I'm tired of fighting my parents, after all these years."

"Have you talked to Lauren lately?"

Nalini shook her head. "Not since Thanksgiving." On more than one occasion, Nalini had picked up her phone to text Lauren and find out how she was doing, only to set it down again without sending a message. The past few weeks had been agonizing, only broken by a different kind of stress: final exams and assignments in the three graduate courses she was taking.

"I hope everything works out for you two. Even if you're getting married, you could still be friends."

"I really would like that, but I can understand why Lauren doesn't want to right now."

Emi stood up and hugged Nalini again. "Well, I'll leave you to it. Have a good trip, Nalini, and I hope you're making the right decision."

Nalini clung to Emi for a moment. "Thanks. I'll see you when I get back."

After Emi had left, Nalini checked her list one more time. With both Emi and Paul traveling home for the holidays, she had decided not to ask Lauren for a ride to Bangor airport, as she'd planned originally before Thanksgiving. Instead, she'd opted for the coastal connection bus service, even though it would add around two hours to her journey.

Each time she'd visited Mumbai previously, she'd been excited about the trip home. This journey, however, held no joy for her. When she'd left India to start school at Wellesley, she knew that the day of reckoning would come. Her parents had never let her forget about the marriage they'd arranged, mentioning it at every opportunity. When the time finally came, with that fateful phone call a few days before Thanksgiving, she'd felt trapped, like a rat in a maze with no exit.

She sighed and rolled her shoulders. It was no use dwelling on it now. She tugged her suitcase off her bed and onto the floor, and left her room. Maybe a walk across campus would help her feel better.

When she headed out to catch the bus the next morning, she had more or less resigned herself to her fate, even if she hadn't really accepted it. She'd been relieved when she'd discovered the convenient campus location for the bus stop, dispelling the unpleasant prospect of dragging her luggage all the way into town.

The bus arrived right on time, and soon Nalini had settled back in her seat, preparing for the two and a half hour trip to Bangor airport. The coach service was scheduled to make quite a few stops along the way, but Nalini didn't mind. As long as the bus kept reasonably close to its planned schedule, it would leave her plenty of time to navigate the unfamiliar airport and catch her flight to Newark.

She'd decided to switch from her customary paperback books to her iPad for the trip, since every bit of space in her luggage was precious. Although she hadn't been too enthused about e-books when she'd first tried the app on her iPad, she had to admit they had their advantages. She still felt a twinge of guilt at buying e-books, though, rather than walking into Great Expectations to feed her reading habit. Of course, trips to the bookstore were likely to be uncomfortable now. Why did things have to be so complicated?

Nalini sighed and shifted in her seat, then opened the e-reader app. Would things ever be the same between her and Lauren? She'd known their relationship was fated to change, but she'd hoped at least they could remain friends. Now, she realized she might have expected too much. She'd tried her best to see things through Lauren's eyes. Although she understood how devastated Lauren had been, a little voice in her head still gave her hope they could be friends again some day, just as Emi had said.

Forcing herself to focus, Nalini turned her attention to her urban fantasy novel. It was a nice change of pace from the more common literary fiction that she enjoyed, although she winced when she remembered that Lauren had recommended the book. Everywhere she turned, she was surrounded by memories of Lauren. After a while, the story sucked her in. She was surprised how quickly the time had passed when the bus pulled into the Bangor airport terminal.

A half-hour later, Nalini was able to resume reading while she waited at the gate for her boarding call. The flight to Newark was uneventful, allowing Nalini to sit back and relax. For no particular reason, she'd been a bit apprehensive about flying in the smaller Embraer jets used by the airline's express service partner.

When she disembarked at Newark, she headed for the nearest food court. The airline peanuts and juice hadn't been enough to dispel her hunger. Fortunately, she had ample time to explore the airport, with more than a six-hour layover. She settled for a Chinese fast-food chain that offered several vegetarian options.

Her hunger sated, Nalini wandered around the airport for another hour before taking the AirTrain to the international terminal for her next flight. Her father's travel agent had booked a nonstop flight from Newark to Mumbai. Spending almost sixteen hours in an airplane wasn't exactly an appealing idea. Maybe a stop halfway to stretch her legs wouldn't have been such a bad thing. Then again, every change of planes mean an opportunity for her luggage to get lost or misdirected, something that seemed to happen with alarming frequency on these intercontinental flights according to her father.

Nalini arrived at her gate, stifled a yawn, and retrieved her iPad from her carry-on bag. She opened her e-book again, but after reading just a few paragraphs, she found her attention wandering once more. For a while, she amused herself by observing the other passengers, making up stories in her head about their backgrounds and final destinations, but her mind kept drifting back to Lauren. She smiled as she recalled the last time she'd woken up next to Lauren, after a night where they'd both had very little sleep. They'd had the best morning sex Nalini had ever experienced.

If Nalini was being honest with herself, she missed the sex, but it wasn't just that. As much as she'd tried to prevent it, to her dismay she realized her feelings for Lauren had grown well beyond friendship. Maybe being over seven thousand miles apart, even it was only for a couple of weeks, would be the cure she needed. It should help her sort out her life, at least. Despite her resolve to put the past behind her, she couldn't help wondering what Lauren was doing at that very moment.

Her hand drifted to the pocket of her jeans, and she retrieved her phone. She swiped through the last photos she had of Lauren, and paused at one that Michelle had taken. Lauren's gorgeous smile made Nalini's heart ache, with the two of them standing, heads together, at the Thanksgiving table. She sat there for a long while, staring at the photo, then opened the messaging app.

Her thumbs skated across the on-screen keyboard. *I'm so sorry for the way we left things. Can we talk?*

She deleted the message without sending it.

When the boarding call finally came, Nalini joined the line at the gate in a daze. She found her seat, tucked her iPad into the seat pocket, stowed her carry-on bag in the overhead bin, and buckled in, all with no clear memory of doing so. It was only when the plane actually started moving that she emerged from her trance and peered out the window.

Once the flight had taken off, she was able to immerse herself in her novel again. It was going to be a long flight, and she didn't want spend the entire journey thinking about Lauren and what might have been. To her relief, after the first meal of the flight was served, she started growing drowsy, and she was finally able to fall asleep.

When Nalini awoke, the cabin lights were still dimmed. A few reading lights cast tight yellow beams here and there, but it seemed that most of the passengers had settled in for the night. At least, night based on the time her flight had left Newark. She stretched and yawned, debating whether to get up and walk the aisles just to get her blood flowing, but a glance at the gently snoring woman and boy in the seats next to her made her rethink her plan. That was the biggest disadvantage of booking a window seat.

With a sigh, she reached for her iPad again. Instead of reading, she occupied herself playing games for the next hour or so until the breakfast service began. As she sipped a steaming cup of coffee, she considered what the next couple of weeks would hold for her. She'd managed to convince herself that she was doing the right thing by going along with her parents' plans. After all, they held the purse strings and, without their financial support, she didn't know if she'd be able to continue her graduate studies. She certainly wouldn't be able to cover any living expenses. But was it worth the price of being married to a man she had no interest in and never would? Even worse, was it worth potentially losing Lauren forever?

By the time the plane landed in Mumbai, Nalini was no closer to a resolution. Her footsteps slowed as she walked toward the immigration checkpoint, and she took several deep breaths as she waited for her turn. When she finally reached the counter, the immigration officer took a cursory look at her documents before stamping her passport and handing it back to her.

She moved on to the luggage claim area, still struggling with opposing emotions. She was happy to be back in the city she still considered home, but the dark cloud of her future hanging over her head dispelled her usual enthusiasm, compared to her last trip a year earlier. She waited at the luggage carousel, elbowing her way through the crowd to grab her bags. The final stop was the customs station, where the line was even longer than at immigration. She mumbled her responses to the officer's questions and sighed with relief when he waved her along without searching her luggage. Then she was free, following the streams of passengers that converged at the exit.

Nalini spotted her parents before they noticed her. When she caught their eye, they began waving frantically, along with dozens of other families gathered at the exit, and she managed a weak smile. Surprising herself, she realized she was actually happy to see them again. She just wished it was under better circumstances.

Her mother was the first to greet her, pulling her into a tight embrace. "You're too thin, Nalu. Must be that American food. Are you eating enough?"

"I'm fine, mom. Really, I am." Eventually, Nalini managed to disentangle herself from her mother's arms, and her father took his turn, giving her a quick hug. Mercifully, he made no comments about her weight.

"Come. The car is waiting." He took her luggage and she followed, her mother bombarding her with questions until they reached the car. The driver jumped out at once and gave her a huge grin before loading her bags into the trunk.

"It is good to see you again, Nalu *memsahib*." The warmth in his eyes helped lift Nalini's spirits just a little. She had known Gopal since she was around five years old, and she was glad to see he was still employed with her family. He was practically a part of it, after all this time.

"I saw you just a year ago, Gopal. It hasn't been that long."

He sighed, shaking his head. "A year is too long. You should visit your family more often." He said that every time she visited.

With a chuckle, Nalini got into the back seat beside her mother. After they left the airport and pulled onto the highway, she steeled herself for the inevitable, endless questions from her mother and discussions about the wedding plans.

To Nalini's surprise, her mother simply patted her knee. "You look so tired, Nalu. I'll let you get some rest on the drive home."

When they reached the luxurious apartment on Nepean Sea Road that Nalini had called home for seventeen years, it was close to midnight. Although she wasn't particularly sleepy, she took the opportunity to go directly to bed, grateful to postpone any conversations about her future until the morning.

TWENTY-TWO

LAUREN CHECKED THE time on her phone, taking a break from reshelving a pile of books that had found their way into the wrong sections. Just fifteen minutes remained until closing time, but she still had work to do.

Despite the way things had ended with Nalini, Lauren still spent way too much time thinking about her. She had maintained radio silence for over three weeks now, and it had been the hardest thing she'd ever done. Her resolve had weakened on occasion when she'd picked up her phone, longing simply to hear Nalini's voice. At those times, she'd reminded herself how much Nalini had hurt her, and that she was doing the right thing.

By now, Nalini was probably somewhere over the Atlantic. Lauren shook her head, angry with herself. It was silly to keep thinking about Nalini like this. When Nalini returned from India, her fate would be sealed. Lauren had tried to consider Nalini's suggestion that they could still be friends. She realized now that she had fallen hopelessly in love with Nalini, and those feelings weren't going to vanish any time soon. How could they be friends, when every time Lauren saw Nalini it would be a reminder of what they could never have?

By the time Lauren closed the store and made it home, she was too exhausted to think about much of anything except crawling into bed. She reminded herself that she had a meeting with Jen before they opened the next morning and checked the alarm on her phone before her head hit the pillow.

Thanks to snoozing her alarm more than once, Lauren still had to rush out the door before sunrise. She even decided to forego her customary cup of coffee and whatever sugary confection Karl and Else had in store for her, walking past the bakery into the back of the bookstore.

Jen was already staring at her computer screen in the office when Lauren arrived and offered a breathless apology for being a few minutes late.

"It's okay, Lauren." Although Jen greeted her warmly enough, she couldn't help noticing the bags under Jen's eyes and Jen's glazed expression. She wondered how early Jen had started her day.

Jen looked up from the screen at last and sighed. "I'll get straight to the point. I had a long phone call with Deanna last night, and the bottom line is that our finances haven't improved. They're actually trending worse than the same quarter last year."

Lauren's heart sank. The book signing had been great, but she'd noticed that the store had been quieter lately. Even Black Friday hadn't been as busy as it normally was.

"I'm going to reevaluate the situation after we do our year-end closing, but I just wanted to give you fair warning." Jen drummed on her desk with a pen. "I had to let Chelsea go, unfortunately. I called her last night after I talked to Deanna. I'll have to cut your hours back next year, Lauren. Worst-case scenario, I may have to let you go, too, and just run the store myself with seasonal help. I'm really sorry."

For a moment, Lauren couldn't believe what she was hearing. The bookstore was the only job she'd known, outside of a short waitressing stint in Orono during her first summer there. To give that up and start over...she tried to wrap her mind around it. On the bright side, at least she wasn't in Chelsea's shoes. Not yet, anyway.

Still, she couldn't think of what she should do next. Maybe she could ask her mother if the grocery store was hiring. Her vision grew blurry, and Jen's voice appeared to be coming from a long distance away. The distant wail of an ambulance siren gave the whole experience a dream-like quality.

Lauren gasped as the siren grew louder. Jen jumped up from her chair and ran to the door. Lauren followed, still in a daze, watching silently as the ambulance pulled up in front of the bakery next door. Two uniformed crew members jumped out, wrestled with a gurney, and pushed it inside.

Jen's face had lost its color. "Oh my god! The Fleischmanns..."

"Should...should we go help?" Lauren managed to find her voice again.

Jen shook her head. "We'd just be in the way." She wrung her hands and began pacing between the door and the counter. "I'll stop by after the ambulance leaves. Why don't you go ahead and get ready to open?"

Somewhere in the back of Lauren's mind, it registered that the bakery had already been open for a couple of hours. Maybe one of their early-morning customers had fallen ill. Lauren couldn't imagine anything happening to Karl or Else. Could the day get any worse?

She went through the routine of opening the store like a robot, her mind wandering back to the interrupted conversation with Jen. Neither of them had the heart to resume the discussion now, and Jen wandered through the aisles while Lauren rearranged the same shelf over and over, until she realized what she was doing. Unexpectedly, her thoughts drifted to Nalini. Despite everything, she wished Nalini was there for her. That would help brighten even the darkest day. Instead, Nalini was on a plane, destined to meet her future husband.

They heard the siren start up again a short while later, and as soon as the ambulance was out of sight, Jen ran outside.

She returned a few moments later. "The place is locked up. No sign of anyone inside."

Lauren's lower lip trembled. Jen placed her hands on Lauren's shoulders. "It'll be okay, Lauren. I'm sure Karl and Else are fine."

Lauren nodded, but she noticed Jen shooting worried glances at the door every few minutes. The bell jangled as the first customer of the day entered the bookstore, and Lauren was thankful for the distraction as she helped the woman locate her favorite author's new release in the cozy mystery section.

It was close to noon when Jen called out to Lauren. Fortunately, there were no customers lingering in the bookstore. Lauren flipped the sign around in the window and locked the door behind her as she followed Jen out.

Karl was sitting at a table near the counter when they entered the bakery. One look at his face told Lauren the worst. She ran across the room and hugged him. His stubble grazed her cheek, and he clung to her, sobbing. Only then did her own tears begin to trickle down her face. Neither of them spoke for a while. Jen soon joined them, her arms encircling them both.

Eventually, Karl's sobs subsided, and he pulled away, returning to his chair. Lauren stepped back and leaned against the counter, not daring to ask the question.

He reached out with a trembling hand, and Jen took it. "My Else. I can't believe she's gone."

Jen hugged him again. "I'm so sorry, Karl."

"It was her heart. There was nothing they could do. I knew she was already gone when the ambulance arrived." He dabbed at his eyes with a napkin. "I was back in the kitchen, and I heard her fall. I called right away. I...I don't know what I'm going to do without her, Jen."

"We'll help you." Lauren cleared her throat. "Whatever you need. We can leave the bookstore closed for a while, can't we, Jen?"

"Of course." Jen stood up. "What's first, Karl?"

He looked up at Jen, then Lauren. "Thank you. I don't really know. There are so many things...but for now, I'll have to shut down the bakery. At least until after..."

"I understand." Jen grabbed her phone. "I'll call the food pantry and see if they can pick up today's stock."

Lauren took Karl's hand. "I can help you in the kitchen."

Putting herself to work made Lauren feel a little better, and she hoped it helped Karl, too. In a few hours, they'd cleaned up the kitchen, stashed away the nonperishable items, and helped a volunteer from the food pantry load up his van.

Jen was back at the bookstore, but Lauren stayed with Karl until he locked up the bakery.

"Are you heading home? I could keep you company, if you're up for it." She wasn't sure how Karl would handle going back to an empty house.

He gave her a tremulous smile. "I appreciate everything you and Jen have done for me. I think I'd like to be alone for a while now."

"Of course. Just call me if you need anything." Lauren hugged him and waited on the sidewalk until his car disappeared around the corner, then she turned and walked into the bookstore. She let out a long, slow breath as Jen squeezed her hand.

Karl and Else were like grandparents to her. She didn't remember much about her own grandparents. Her father's parents had never been close to Lauren or her mother, and both her mother's parents had died relatively young. It had left a void in her life that she hadn't quite acknowledged until she was older. She still remembered the three-layer cake Else had baked and decorated, as lavish as any wedding cake, when she left Zachary for college. Her mother had saved some in the freezer and, although Lauren hadn't thought about it for a while, she wished she still had a piece stashed away.

When Lauren got home that night, her mother was still at the grocery store. Lauren thought about texting her to let her know about Else but decided against it. That was the kind of news best delivered in person.

She scrolled through her messages and tapped on her last conversation with Nalini. Of all the women in the world, she had to fall for someone who had agreed to an arranged marriage—with a man. Obviously, if Nalini had felt the same way about Lauren, she would never have left for India to oblige her parents. There were times when Lauren had dared to hope that Nalini shared her feelings. On those occasions, she sensed that Nalini had let her guard down just a little, and she thought she'd glimpsed something stronger than friendship in Nalini's eyes.

Had she been mistaken?

TWENTY-THREE

WHEN THE MORNING sunlight flooded Nalini's bedroom, she awoke surprisingly refreshed after her long journey. She couldn't remember dreaming at all, but she had clearly managed to get some sleep. She lay in bed for a while, looking around the room that had been hers all through her childhood. The walls were still adorned with framed photographs from her father's trips to exotic locations around the country. He had been an enthusiastic amateur photographer when she was a child, still clinging to the use of photographic film when the world had largely gone digital. Nalini wondered if he still maintained his hobby. She'd heard little of it during her last trip to India, and she knew he didn't travel as much as he used to.

With a sigh, she swung her legs over the edge of the bed. Her suitcase lay on the floor, still untouched. She unzipped it and rummaged through the pile of clothes, searching for a package of disposable contact lenses, when her fingers brushed against something cold and smooth.

She picked it up at once, recognizing it by touch, and brought it to her lips. Memories of her day with Lauren at Agate Beach came flooding back, and she stroked the gray banded stone with one finger. That had been one of the best days of her life—getting to know Lauren and enjoying the beauty of their surroundings at the same time.

Tears spilled from her eyes as her grip tightened on the agate. She missed Lauren more than ever. How could she go through with this marriage? She had already destroyed her chances with Lauren, but maybe it wasn't too late to salvage her own life.

A quick shower helped improve her mood. As she dressed, her resolution to take charge of her own destiny grew stronger. She walked into the dining room, where her parents were still eating breakfast.

"Nalu! Come, sit." Her mother hugged her tight. "I didn't want to wake you earlier. I'll get you some coffee. I know how you used to start your day with a cup before you'd eaten anything. It always seemed strange to me, but..."

Nalini remained standing and placed a hand on her mother's arm, stemming the flow of words. "I have something to tell you."

"What is it? Why don't you eat something first?" Her father finally looked up from the daily newspaper that he always read at breakfast.

Nalini took a deep breath. "I can't go ahead with this wedding. I can't marry Nikhil. I...I'm gay."

"What do you mean?" Her mother's voice raised in pitch. "I don't understand."

"I'm a lesbian, mom. I like women. Not men."

A high-pitched wail erupted from her mother's throat. "Nalu, please. Don't talk such rubbish. We didn't raise you that way. Of course you will marry Nikhil. The arrangements are already made, and we just—"

"It's got nothing to do with how I was raised. I've known this for a long time. I just didn't tell you before, because I was afraid you would behave like...well, exactly like you're behaving now." Nalini bit her lip.

Her mother groaned and clutched her head. "Why, Nalu? Why are you doing this, after all we've done for you? Besides, this marriage isn't just about you. It's a great opportunity for your father's business. Nikhil's father is willing to go into a partnership once the wedding plans are settled."

"Yes, I'm sure that's important." Nalini braced herself and tried to ignore the sound of her blood roaring in her ears. "Of course, a business deal is more valuable than your daughter's happiness."

Her father hadn't said a word. As Nalini turned to him, he tossed his newspaper onto the table, and it slid to the floor. He pushed his chair back and stood up. "Get out!"

"What?" Nalini's eyes began to sting. "Dad, please listen to me. I can't change who I am."

He pointed to the door. "Get out. You are no longer our daughter."

The tears came freely now, and Nalini dabbed at her eyes with the sleeve of her *kurta*. "But...where will I go? Surely you don't mean this?"

"It's not our concern where you go. You are not part of this family, and we will never send you another cent to support your filthy, perverted lifestyle." He walked to the door and opened it. "Go. Now!"

"Nalu...please." Her mother reached out, sobbing, but Nalini was already halfway through the door. She turned her head, took a last look at her childhood home, and strode down the hallway to the elevator. The door slammed behind her.

She emerged in the lavishly decorated, marble-lined lobby, her vision still clouded by tears. What on earth was she going to do? She had no money with her, and all her belongings were still in her luggage. Fortunately, her phone was in the pocket of her shorts. She wiped away her tears with her sleeve and flipped through her phone contacts. There was only one person she could turn to, at this point.

A half-hour later, a car pulled up outside the entrance to the neighborhood park at the end of the street. Nalini jumped up from the bench where she'd been seated, playing games on her phone to distract herself from the sobering reality of what had just happened.

"Nalini, what's going on?"

She embraced Ravi, fighting back tears again. "I'm so glad I was able to reach you."

"Let's get in the car, and you can tell me everything on the way."

In a few minutes, Ravi had eased into the never-ending chaos of Mumbai traffic, and Nalini had recovered enough to relate her experience without breaking down again. Ravi listened without interrupting, but his expression grew darker.

"I can't believe your parents would do such a thing. Although, based on my own experience, I'm not entirely surprised."

"I knew you'd understand." Ravi hadn't changed much since their junior college years. Nalini felt bad that she hadn't been able to see him on her last visit to Mumbai, but they'd kept in touch through e-mail and WhatsApp. Now, it seemed as if the past few years had vanished, and she was back in junior college with her best friend again.

"Look, you can stay with us as long as you want. No point spending money on a hotel. We have a spare bedroom, and I know Gautam would love to see you again after all this time."

"How are the two of you doing?" She felt somewhat ashamed that she hadn't asked Ravi that to begin with.

He smiled. "Better than ever. His parents actually came around after the first year. They don't visit us, but at least they're speaking to him again."

"And yours?" She was almost afraid to ask.

"The less said, the better." His smile vanished. "Anyway, what about your stuff? I assume it's all still in your parents' apartment?"

Nalini nodded.

"I know they won't even let me in to their place, but you could try calling Sanjeev. Maybe he can talk to them and convince them to see reason, although it won't be easy. At least, not for a while."

She brightened up a bit at that prospect. If anything, Sanjeev's parents were even more conservative than hers, but her cousin had charmed his way into Nalini's family at an early age. Sometimes, Nalini wondered if they saw him as the son they'd desperately wanted but never had. Maybe Ravi was right. "I'll talk to Sanjeev when we get to your apartment. My phone is nearly out of charge."

As Ravi had predicted, Nalini received a warm welcome from Gautam when they arrived at the apartment, a modest two-bedroom unit in a newer development along Worli Sea Face. She knew that both men were among the few people in the world who could truly relate to her experience, and their kind words did much to console her.

She called her cousin shortly thereafter, and he promised to stop by and talk to her parents that morning. Ravi and Gautam convinced Nalini to join them for a late breakfast at a nearby South Indian restaurant. Sitting there, sipping coffee so hot it scorched her tongue and devouring a generous serving of onion *uttapam*, she almost felt as if she'd entered an alternate reality. She was so glad she'd turned to Ravi for help.

A few hours later, Sanjeev showed up. He wheeled Nalini's bags inside and pulled her into his arms.

"I'm so sorry," he whispered over and over again. "I tried to talk some sense into them, but you know how stubborn your father gets. Give it some time. At least they let me bring your luggage here. I have a feeling it would have ended up in the trash if I hadn't intervened."

"Thank you, Sanjeev." Nalini flopped down on the sofa and buried her head in her hands.

"I'll keep trying," he said. "Let me know if there's anything else I can do."

After her cousin left, Nalini began unpacking her bags. She set the piece of agate on the nightstand by the bed after rolling it between her fingers, struggling with her instinct to text Lauren and tell her everything that had happened.

She resisted the urge. Although she had avoided a disastrous marriage, Nalini had no idea what the future would hold for her. How would she support herself through graduate school without her parents' financial help? It wasn't like she could find a job—her student visa eliminated that possibility. Her teaching assistantship included a tuition waiver, but the meager stipend it offered wouldn't be enough to cover her living expenses, especially the graduate student dorm fees.

Most of all, she knew how upset Lauren had been when they'd parted ways. Nalini had no right to expect that Lauren would simply take her back and forgive everything, even if she managed to find a way out of her dire financial straits.

Suddenly, Nalini realized that it wasn't her financial situation that upset her the most. She could even face abandoning her graduate studies and staying in India if she had to. What hurt the most was that she might never get to see Lauren again.

TWENTY-FOUR

S NOW WAS FALLING in thick, wet flakes as Lauren and her mother pulled into the driveway of McIverson Funeral Home. It had taken some persuasion on Lauren's part to convince her mother to attend the service. The last time they had both set foot in the small, family-owned funeral home was four years earlier, for Luke's memorial service. A solitary wreath on the front door was their only reminder that it was three days to Christmas. At first, Lauren thought Karl might have waited until after the holidays to hold the service, but Jen had told her he'd wanted to make the arrangements as soon as possible. The Christmas season had always been Lauren's favorite time of year but, this year, the holidays held little joy for her.

Lauren was thankful that they didn't have to deal with a church service. There were no Lutheran churches in Zachary or the surrounding towns. Karl and Else were born and raised in the Lutheran church, but after they'd settled in Zachary, they had only infrequently attended Sunday services at the local congregational church.

They were escorted into the visitation room by Benny McIverson, whom Lauren had known since middle school. He seated them two rows behind Karl, who was talking to a man that Lauren didn't recognize but who bore a faint resemblance to Else. She knew that neither of the Fleischmanns had family in Zachary, but it was possible that a relative had managed to make it out to Zachary on short notice.

"Should we?" Her mother stood up, and Lauren nodded. They walked to the front of the room. Lauren embraced Karl and managed to fight back her tears as he clung to her. When he finally let her go, Karl gestured to the man standing beside him.

"This is Werner, Else's cousin from Augusta. Werner, these are two of my dearest friends, Lauren and Michelle Clarke. Lauren works at the bookstore that I was telling you about."

"I'm so sorry for your loss." The words came automatically from Lauren's mouth as she gripped Werner's hand. She had never been comfortable at funerals, and she'd always been awkward around the subject of death. Having Luke's life cut short at the age of twenty-three hadn't helped, either.

"Thank you," Werner said. "Karl has told me of your kindness in his time of need. I'm so glad he has the support of friends."

Still struggling to hold it together, Lauren took her mother's hand and proceeded to the casket. Else looked peaceful, and Lauren stood there for a while, wishing she had been around to comfort Else in her last moments.

As if she knew exactly what Lauren was thinking, her mother spoke up. "There wasn't anything you could have done, Lauren. I know how much she cared for you."

"It's just...I have no idea what Karl is going to do without her." Lauren sniffled as they walked back to their seats. "Else was the heart and soul of the bakery. Karl loves the place, too, but it was always Else's dream."

"He'll figure something out." Her mother patted Lauren's hand.

The service was mercifully brief. After Else's casket had been removed to begin the final journey to the crematorium, Lauren and her mother lingered in the foyer of the funeral home with a few of the other guests. She spotted Jen talking to Josh and waved to them. Before she could join them, someone laid a hand on her shoulder, and Lauren spun around.

"Karl! I thought you'd left already." Although Karl looked like he hadn't slept all night, Lauren thought he was holding it together pretty well.

"I was about to. I just wanted to see if you could meet me at the bakery tomorrow morning. There's something I'd like to discuss."

"Of course. I'll be at the bookstore all day, so just stop by whenever you're ready."

Karl gave her a gentle smile and squeezed her shoulder.

It wasn't until Lauren got home that the emotion of the funeral caught up with her. She already missed Else more than she had realized, and she sank down on her bed, holding her head in her hands.

If only Nalini was here...she had to stop thinking about that. As she'd done several times over the past few days, Lauren scrolled through the photos on her phone. Why had she ever agreed to their silly friends-with-benefits arrangement to begin with? Nalini had just set her up for disappointment.

No, that wasn't strictly true. Nalini had been up front with her, telling her that a long-term relationship was out of the question. It was Lauren's own foolishness that led her to believe there could be something more. She only had herself to blame for letting her feelings get the better of her, for falling in love with a woman she couldn't have...

She glanced at the miniature Christmas village on her desk. She'd had the set of ceramic houses and tiny figurines since she was five years old, and setting it up the day after Thanksgiving had been a tradition for her ever since then. Even when she was away in college, her mother had taken over arranging it in Lauren's room and had sent her pictures.

Her eyes misted over as she retrieved the box from her closet. Slowly, she unplugged the lights and restored each piece to its place in the box.

The next morning, she had to drag herself out of bed in order to get to the bookstore on time. Jen gave her a hug as soon as she walked in the door. For the next few hours, Lauren went through the motions of shelving the new stock. Holiday romances were still popular, and Lauren expected they'd move a good number of them through early January.

Just before noon, Karl stuck his head through the door, and Lauren followed him back to the bakery. His tone was subdued, but he'd regained some of his former energy as he made small talk about the holidays when they were both seated at a table.

"I hate to close up during the holidays," he said, waving a hand, "but I just couldn't manage it by myself."

"I understand." Lauren squeezed his hand. "Anyone would, given your circumstances. You shouldn't feel bad about your decision."

"That's why I wanted to talk to you today. You see, Else and I had several discussions about the future of the bakery and what would happen when she...when we were no longer able to take care of things around here."

Lauren gulped. This wasn't quite the conversation she'd imagined having with Karl, but if it helped him to talk about it, she was willing to be his sounding board. She'd assumed they'd just sell the bakery and retire, although it would be hard for them to let go of something that had been in their blood for so many years. Now that Else was gone, she wondered if Karl would feel guilty about selling.

"We came to an agreement that was an easy decision for both of us." Karl leaned forward, rubbing the stubble on his chin. "Lauren, Else wanted you to have the bakery, and I agreed. It's yours to do with as you wish. I would like it if you kept the place open, of course, but if you choose to sell it, that's okay, too."

Lauren gasped. "Me? But I don't know the first thing about running a bakery. What would I do? What about your families? Surely there must be someone else who..."

"You can learn. I would stay involved until you picked up the basics, and you could always hire someone to help you after that. We're small, but we're doing well enough financially. Else made some smart choices about limiting our growth, and it paid off in the end." Karl took a sip from his coffee. "And family isn't an issue, really. The only close family Else had is Werner, and he wants nothing to do with the bakery. He's doing quite well for himself, with his insurance company in Augusta."

"I don't know what to say." Lauren ran her fingers through her hair. "I really don't know. I mean, I'm happy that you and Else thought so much of me, but I'm not sure if I can handle this."

"You don't have to decide right now." Karl patted her hand. "I'll keep the place closed until we have a plan in place. As I said, if you choose not to run the bakery yourself, you could still sell it and keep the proceeds."

"But...what will you do, Karl? For money, I mean."

He smiled, his eyes shining. "Don't worry about me. I've invested wisely over the years, and it's time I slowed down. I love this place, but I'm an old man, and I really could use some time to myself. If you do take it over, I'll be happy knowing it's in good hands." He leaned forward. "Else knew how much you wanted to finish college. Maybe you could still do that once you get the bakery up and running."

Lauren had a lot to think about as she walked home that night. She'd decided not to say anything to Jen until she'd figured out things for herself. Her mother was working late again, so Lauren had the house to herself while she reheated leftovers and opened her laptop at the kitchen table.

She began scrolling through the web pages for the university's returning students program. All this time, she'd imagined herself majoring in English literature, if she was ever able to continue her studies. Now, she realized it was simply the default path she'd chosen because she enjoyed writing. However, her conversations with Alyssa Forester—whose college major was accounting and finance, of all things—had convinced her that you didn't need a fancy degree to be a writer.

By the time she'd finished dinner, she'd checked out every course in the business management program. Her heart beat faster as she read through the application forms. Was she really going to do this? With a sigh, she closed the browser window. She wasn't ready...yet.

She loved working at Great Expectations, but her recent discussions with Jen had reminded her that there were no guarantees in life when it came to employment, or anything else. She had to choose her own path. From the financial statements Karl had given her, she knew that the income from the bakery would more than cover her college costs. She could take part-time classes to start with.

She ran her fingers over the leather-bound classics on the bookshelf in the living room. Leaving the bookstore would hurt, and leaving Jen would hurt even more, but at least she'd be right next door. Managing a bakery wasn't something she had ever contemplated as a career, but Karl was right. She could learn. It would be foolish to waste the opportunity. And maybe, once she was done with college, she would finally have more time to take her writing career seriously. Even Alyssa Forester had started out as a writer with a day job.

If only there was a way to stay involved with the bookstore and still keep the bakery. That would be the best of both worlds.

TWENTY-FIVE

MERRY CHRISTMAS, NALINI!" Ravi gave her a hug that nearly squeezed all the breath from her lungs, and Gautam followed up with a gentler but still warm embrace. The two of them stood back, smiling, and Ravi held out a rectangular, gift-wrapped package.

Nalini gasped. "You really didn't need to get me anything. You've done so much for me already. I don't know what I would have done without both of you."

She sat down on the sofa. As a child, Christmas had been a big deal, even for her traditional Hindu family. Many of her school friends had celebrated Christmas, regardless of their religious backgrounds. What could be better than a day filled with gifts, tons of food, and family gatherings? Despite her still-simmering anger at the way her parents had treated her, Nalini had to admit she missed being with them on Christmas morning.

"Go ahead, open it." The smile on Ravi's face grew even broader.

For a moment, Nalini frowned. "I'm really sorry. I didn't have a chance to get you two anything."

"Don't worry about us." Gautam sat down beside her. "We're just glad you're here."

Gingerly, Nalini slid her thumb under an opening in the gift wrap. Then, dispensing with caution, she ripped off the rest of the colorful tartan paper to reveal a hardback edition of *The Namesake*, Jhumpa Lahiri's first novel.

"Thank you," she whispered. She didn't have the heart to tell them that she already owned all of Lahiri's books. They occupied pride of place on the small shelf in her dorm room, back in Zachary.

Ravi patted her on the shoulder. "Take a look inside."

She flipped the cover open and there, on the half-title page, was an inscription and signature from the author.

"Oh my god! Ravi, I can't accept this." Nalini tried to hand the book back to him, but he pushed her hands away.

"I want you to have it. I got her to sign it a few years ago, when she did an Indian book tour and visited Nalanda here in Mumbai. To be honest, I'm not as devoted a fan as you are. I know you'll appreciate it a lot more than I did."

Nalini hugged him. "This is so awesome." For a short while, she could set aside the nerve-wracking doubts about her future and just enjoy the spirit of the holidays.

Ravi and Gautam convinced her to accompany them on a morning walk along Worli Sea Face. As the distinctive, salty tang of the air permeated her senses, her thoughts went back to that memorable day at Agate Beach. She reached into the pocket of her jeans and rubbed the smooth stone. She carried it wherever she went now, a little piece of what she and Lauren once had.

Could they ever have that again?

"Nalini, I meant to tell you earlier." Ravi's voice broke into her thoughts. "I talked to my friend in the airlines, and he confirmed that your return ticket is still good. Your parents didn't cancel it."

Nalini let out a breath. "Thanks. That's a relief. At least now I know I can get back, although I'm not sure what I'm going to do once I'm there. My teaching assistantship takes care of my tuition for next semester, but my dorm fees are still due, and I really don't have any money saved."

They had reached the entrance to the Bandra-Worli Sea Link, and Nalini paused to take in the view of the imposing cable-stayed bridge. Ravi stopped beside her, and they turned to lean against the concrete barrier, facing the waves. She swung her feet over the wall and sat there, watching the few small boats in the distance being tossed by the waves. Her two friends soon joined her, and Ravi cleared his throat.

"Nalini, Gautam and I talked about this yesterday, and...well, we would like to lend you the money."

Nalini glanced at Ravi, her eyes opening wide. "That's really sweet of you, but I can't take your money." She wasn't sure how Ravi and Gautam were doing financially. Although they were both in the software industry and worked at the same company, she knew how expensive rents were in this part of the city. She couldn't ask them to make such a huge sacrifice for her. They argued about it for a while, but Ravi finally relented, much to Nalini's relief.

When they returned to the apartment, Nalini offered to help out in the kitchen.

"Don't worry. We can take care of everything," Ravi said. "Just relax and enjoy some quiet time if you want, or you can watch TV. Do you still follow cricket? The first Australia-India one-day match is probably on now."

She grinned. "I'm not sure I'd be much help anyway, unless you want something heated in the microwave. As for cricket, I never really had the opportunity to keep up with it after I left home. I couldn't even tell you who most of the players are on the Indian team now."

Before long, Nalini had curled up on the sofa in front of the TV. After flipping through the channels for a while, she turned on the cricket match after all and reached for her phone.

Maybe she should text Lauren and give her an update on everything that had happened. That would be a long text conversation, however. Besides, it was quite likely that Lauren didn't even want to hear from her at this point. Lauren certainly had made no attempt to contact her.

As good as it felt to be back in Mumbai, there was nothing really here for Nalini now. She wondered if she should change her ticket and leave earlier. Her original departure was scheduled for January 8. Although she enjoyed spending time with Ravi and Gautam, she would rather get back to Zachary and figure out what she was going to do with her life. She'd have to stay enrolled in graduate school, or else her visa would lapse and she'd have to return to India—this time, not by choice.

Should she try calling Lauren to explain everything? She wasn't confident that Lauren would answer her call. She would give anything right now to feel Lauren's fingers running through her hair, Lauren's warm breath against her cheek, Lauren's soft lips against hers...

With a sigh, she turned back to her phone. She would wait until she returned to Zachary. Her chest tightened with the realization of how much she missed Lauren. But it was more than just missing her best friend, she now realized. Despite her best efforts to stay unattached, had she fallen in love with Lauren?

As she scrolled mindlessly through her social media apps, Ravi came into the room and sat next to her. Nalini seized the chance to discuss the change in her travel plans with him.

"You know, you can stay here as long as you like," he said, although his attention was focused on the screen as another Indian wicket fell.

"I'm so grateful for everything you and Gautam have done, but I really need to get back. There are some...issues I need to resolve, and the sooner I do that, the better."

"I understand. I'll call my friend at the airlines tomorrow. I'm sure he can figure something out." Ravi glanced at her phone, and Nalini realized she still had her Facebook app open, with a picture of her and Lauren displayed prominently in a post from a month earlier. "Tell me about her. Is she the reason you want to return early?"

"Maybe." Nalini dropped the phone in her lap and threw up her hands. "I don't know. She may not even want to talk to me."

"Why? What happened?"

Nalini sighed. "It's a long story." She took a deep breath and dived into the tale of how she'd met Lauren, how they'd agreed on their friends-with-benefits arrangement, and everything else that had followed.

When she was done, Ravi frowned. "I don't see the problem, though. You're not marrying Nikhil now. You should be free to pursue a relationship with Lauren."

"It's not that simple." Nalini's hand shook as she picked up her phone again, idly swiping through photos of Lauren. "She thought I was a coward for not defying my parents earlier and being with her. I ended our arrangement, because I didn't want her to get too close to me, and I may have ended our friendship, too."

"Do you love her?"

Nalini remained silent for several moments. She had tried so hard to keep Lauren at arm's length. Of course, the sex had been great, but now all she could think of was the way that Lauren's eyes sparkled when she talked about her favorite books, and how her cheeks turned an adorable shade of pink when Nalini caught her off guard with a particularly salacious comment. She even treasured the times they'd spent together not saying a word, but just being there in the moment.

"I really tried to keep my feelings in check," she said, her voice dropping to a whisper. "I didn't want to get into a relationship that I knew would have no chance of success. I should have known better. Yes, I love her, and I can't imagine going back to a life without her."

"Have you told her that?"

Nalini could only shake her head. After Ravi returned to the kitchen, she sat staring at the TV screen but not processing any of what was happening in the game. She did love Lauren, and now she wished she'd realized it sooner. Maybe she could still salvage their relationship. She would return to Zachary, apologize, and tell Lauren how she felt in person. As much as she longed to hear Lauren's voice, this was something she didn't want to do over the phone.

Her spirits lifted the next day when Ravi confirmed her new travel arrangements.

"The only flight that he could get you on leaves around 1:00 a.m. on the thirty-first," Ravi said. "With the time difference, it will be around noon on the same day when you get into Bangor. If you're not too jet-lagged, you'll still have plenty of time to celebrate."

"That's fine." Nalini was just glad she'd be on her way back earlier than planned. "I'm not a big fan of New Year's Eve parties, anyway. Maybe I'll just sleep in, for once."

In less than a week, she'd be able to see Lauren again. Assuming, of course, that Lauren would want to see her.

TWENTY-SIX

LAUREN WOKE TO the rich aroma of dark roast coffee and realized it was one of those rare mornings when her mother didn't have to go into work. She yawned and stretched, glancing out the window at the six inches of snow that still remained from the last storm. Normally, she'd be pleased with a white Christmas but, this year, the holiday lacked its customary appeal.

By the time she made her way into the kitchen, the scent of coffee mingled with that of bacon and eggs. Her mother was seated at the kitchen island with a mug of coffee. She got up and gave Lauren a quick hug.

"Merry Christmas, Lauren. Here, have a seat, and I'll get you some breakfast."

"It smells great," Lauren said, still yawning. "Merry Christmas, mom."

"It's so rare that I get a chance to cook breakfast anymore." Her mother heaped a plate with scrambled eggs and several strips of bacon, added two slices of toast, and set it in front of Lauren. "I have to say I'm glad we decided to scale back our meal plans this year, though."

Lauren nodded. "I just didn't feel like it."

"I understand completely." Her mother refilled her coffee mug and reclaimed her seat. "Have you decided what you're going to do about the bakery?"

Lauren had dropped the bombshell a couple of nights earlier, and although her mother had been as surprised as Lauren had when Karl broke the news, she'd promised to leave the decision up to Lauren.

"Not yet, but I've been thinking about it a lot." Lauren sighed with satisfaction after the first mouthful of scrambled eggs. "Selling the bakery would really help us out financially, but I feel like I'd be letting Else down. She loved that place, and it was her whole life. I still can't believe all of this is happening."

"Think about your own future, Lauren. Don't worry about me and my finances. I know you've always wanted to go back to college and get a place of your own. That takes money." She raised her hands. "Sorry, I didn't mean to interfere. I'm going to clean up and start working on the turkey. Will Josh be stopping by later?"

"He's counting on it. I haven't seen him in a while, but I texted him last night, and he confirmed." It was something of a holiday tradition. Josh spent the day with his parents and usually came over to visit Lauren and her mother in the evening, helping them work their way through leftovers.

Although their meal preparations were more modest than usual, the morning passed quickly. Lauren managed to keep herself occupied enough that she didn't really have a chance to think about Nalini until she was slumped on the couch after the meal. Instinctively, she recalled how happy she'd been on Thanksgiving, snuggled up against Nalini on this very couch, before everything had fallen apart later that night. She couldn't help wondering what Nalini's Christmas was like in India. Would she be spending it with her future husband and his family?

When Josh arrived, Lauren was in somewhat better spirits, and she managed a smile while they exchanged gifts. For some time now, she and Josh had set strict dollar limits for each other. Lauren grinned when she opened hers. Josh was nothing if not predictable. She lifted the lid from the sampler box of hand-crafted chocolates, from a store just north of Zachary, and bit into a hazelnut creme.

Of course, it wasn't like she'd needed to do a lot of shopping, either. Josh wasn't much of a reader, but he had developed a fascination with biographies ever since high school, especially ones related to the music industry. Knowing his tastes well, Lauren had selected a book about Leonard Cohen from the discount shelf at the bookstore.

After they'd each grabbed a plate of leftovers and were gathered around the dinner table, Lauren gave Josh the news about the bakery. He almost dropped the chunk of turkey that he'd raised to his mouth when she mentioned what the place was worth, based on the last appraisal Karl had done.

"That's amazing, Lauren!" He put down his fork. "So, you've decided to sell?"

She shook her head. "I haven't decided anything yet. Karl told me to take my time, but I know he'd like to finalize the arrangements soon."

Josh glanced at Lauren's mother, who shrugged. After dinner was done, and they'd settled down in front of the TV, Josh revealed a surprise of his own.

"You remember that friend of Kevin's who had connections with an indie label? Well, they listened to our demo, and they want to sign us for one album to start with."

Lauren dropped the TV remote and hugged him. "Josh! That's fantastic!" Her mother jumped up and embraced Josh, too, much to Lauren's surprise. Lauren's mother had never made it out to any of the shows that the band played in town, but Lauren had convinced her how much music meant to Josh. He'd always maintained he was a musician with a day job.

Josh grinned. "The funny thing is...it was something Nalini said that helped. You know how she was kidding you about Harry Styles? Well, at the last minute, I decided to include a cover of

'Sign of the Times.' We'd recorded it a few weeks earlier, and I think it was the only time we got a song down on the first take."

Lauren hadn't heard the band cover that song, but she knew Josh certainly had the vocal range to pull it off.

"Kevin's guy said nobody besides Harry could ever do that song justice," Josh continued, "but I guess we came pretty close. Of course, our album will be mostly original songs with maybe one or two covers, but the label liked what they heard. We'll still be responsible for a lot of the legwork ourselves, including social media promotion and other marketing, but it's a start."

"I'm so happy for you." Lauren stood up. "And I haven't forgotten our deal. Actually, I began checking into it a few days ago." She went to her bedroom and returned with her laptop. She flipped it open and explained to her mother that she'd finally decided to finish up her college classes here in Zachary, rather than applying to the main campus in Orono where she'd started.

Her mother nodded. "I know it's been hard on you all this time, Lauren, especially when I was such a mess after Luke died. I'd hoped you could continue your studies some day, and I'm really proud of you for taking such a big step."

"Thanks, mom." Lauren pulled up the page for the business school and sidled closer to Josh.

"I suppose you'll want to get your own place, too." Her mother looked down for a moment.

"I...let's see how that goes." Lauren knew that things weren't as bad for her mother as they were a few years earlier, but she was right. Going back to college was a huge deal. "This is for the fall semester, so we still have some time to work out the details. Assuming I get into the program, that is."

"I'm sure you'll get in." Josh leaned over to peer at the screen. "How come you're looking at business majors, though? I always thought you wanted to get a literature degree."

"Times change." Lauren downloaded the application form, saved it on the desktop, and took a deep breath. "I'll still take some literature classes, but this degree will help in the long run, whether I'm running the bakery or working somewhere else."

Her mother came over and took Lauren's hands in hers. "I hope you don't burn yourself out, what with college and trying to work full time, too. You know I'll support you in whatever you do."

"If I keep the bakery, I'm sure I can hire someone to run the day-to-day business, and I'll only be taking some evening classes the first year." Lauren closed the laptop. "I'll get the application done tomorrow. I know it sounds like a lot, but I really want to do this."

Josh put his arm around her and squeezed her shoulder. "If there's anything I can do to help, let me know."

"Just don't forget me when you're famous and touring all over the country."

Josh chuckled. "I don't think we have to worry about that just yet."

A good night's sleep brought the clarity that Lauren needed, and when she got out of bed, she'd made up her mind about her plan. Before she headed out to open the bookstore the next morning, Lauren called Karl and told him she was going to keep the bakery. The excitement in his voice reinforced her conviction that she'd made the right choice. She agreed to meet him after her shift at the bookstore to go over the details. Now, she had to break the news to Jen.

"I hate to lose my best employee, but I understand." To Lauren's relief, Jen hugged her after she'd explained the situation. "With the uncertainty about the store's future, I can't really blame you for taking another opportunity when it lands right in your lap like this. Besides, you'll just be next door, so we can still hang out whenever you want."

"Actually, that's part of what I wanted to discuss." Lauren tapped her fingers on the counter. "I've been developing some ideas about a few changes to the bakery. I'd like to make it a bit more upscale and give it a coffee shop vibe. We don't really have a decent coffee shop in Zachary, unless you count the cheap coffee at the gas station out near Cooper's. It could be a great draw, especially during the tourist season. And that got me thinking. What do all the chain bookstores have that we don't?"

Jen inhaled sharply. "I see where you're going with this. Do you think it would work?"

"We won't know until we try, but I do think it could help the bookstore. I even thought about putting in a door so we could connect the two stores. And I might still be able to cover an occasional shift in the bookstore if you need me. Of course, I have to discuss all this with Karl later today, but I don't think he'll have a problem with it."

"You're going to be taking on so many new responsibilities, Lauren, but it's worth doing if it makes you happy." Jen pursed her lips. "Now that I think about it, why don't you give Chelsea a call? She used to work in a coffee shop when she was in Portland. I really liked her, and I hated that I had to let her go. Maybe you could use her experience."

"Thanks, Jen." The doorbell interrupted her, and Lauren spun around, preparing to greet their first customer of the day. "I know it's a lot, but I'm ready for a new chapter in my life. And I'll definitely talk to Chelsea. I enjoyed working with her, too."

There was only more thing that would make Lauren's happiness complete, but that dream had evaporated when Nalini had left for India.

TWENTY-SEVEN

N ALINI STIFLED A yawn as she walked down the jet bridge. She was glad to be back on American soil, but she hadn't managed to sleep at all during the sixteen-hour flight from Mumbai to Newark. She might be able to take a nap after she'd located her gate for the connection to Bangor, but she'd probably be overwhelmed with paranoia about missing her flight.

She managed to navigate through the formalities of immigration and customs without incident. As she'd done on her previous trip, Nalini opted to take the AirTrain to the gate for her connection. When she arrived and settled in for the four-hour layover, she pulled her phone from her pocket and realized it was still in airplane mode. She rarely used the airlines' expensive WiFi during a flight, spending her time reading or playing offline games instead. She activated the connection and frowned when she checked her messages. There was one from the coach service regarding the change she'd made to her original return date, advising her to call them as soon as possible.

It was just before six in the morning, so she didn't think the office would be open yet. She called the number anyway, expecting to leave a message, but was surprised when someone answered. She gave them her information and waited on hold for a while.

"I'm sorry, madam, but you were waitlisted due to the change in your return date." The woman on the line sounded more bored than sorry. "We have limited service today, due to weather conditions, and I strongly recommend that you make alternative arrangements. We can't guarantee a seat when you arrive in Bangor."

Just what she needed. Nalini hung up, not even bothering to ask if she'd get a partial refund of her round-trip fare. She slumped back in her seat and checked the weather app on her phone. Heavy snow was in the forecast for downeast Maine, with over a foot expected in Bangor and even more along the coast. It was due to start around the time her flight landed, so she hoped she wouldn't run into any delays. It looked like the heaviest snow would begin falling around noon, so she could understand why bus service would be affected, but it still annoyed her. She wished she wasn't so exhausted. Her brain would probably deal with this setback better if she'd gotten some sleep.

She weighed her options. She hated using ride-sharing services and hadn't even installed the apps on her phone, but maybe this was one situation where they could be useful. She'd feel so much better if someone was waiting for her at the airport, though. Someone she knew and trusted, rather than a total stranger. Unfortunately, both Paul and Emi were still away for the holidays, leaving one other option that she hesitated to consider.

Nalini took a deep breath, brought up her favorites list, and tapped Lauren's number. She cleared her throat. The phone rang a few times.

"Hello, Lauren? I'm sorry for waking you."

"Nalini? Where are you?"

Nalini heaved a sigh of relief. At least Lauren hadn't rejected her call. She could sense the sleepiness in Lauren's tone, and she wondered if she'd made the right decision. Once she began explaining her dilemma, though, Lauren appeared to be more alert.

"Text me when you get your luggage, and I'll swing by the passenger pickup area." Lauren hadn't asked her anything beyond her flight's expected time of arrival in Bangor, and Nalini was relieved. She needed to tell Lauren everything that had happened in Mumbai, but that could wait. Maybe the ride back to Zachary would be a good opportunity to get things back on track. If that was what Lauren wanted, of course. Otherwise, it would be a long, awkward ride, but Nalini was beyond caring at this point. She just wanted to get back to Zachary and go to bed, while she still had one. Fortunately, her dorm fees weren't due until the first week of classes, so she had a small grace period to figure out how to pay her bill. She'd never liked carrying a balance on her credit card, but that seemed like her only option for now.

Just hearing Lauren's voice had eased Nalini's stress levels, though, and she resolved not to worry about her finances until she'd caught up with her sleep. She looked around the gate. Across from her, a young couple wrestled with a girl who must have been four or five years old. She wriggled across her mother's lap, squealing.

The girl spotted Nalini and came running over before her parents could say a word.

"Hello," she said, sticking out her hand. "I'm Kendra."

Despite her fatigue, Nalini couldn't help smiling. "It's nice to meet you, Kendra. I'm Nalini. Do you live in Bangor?"

The girl nodded. "My daddy is a professor at the university. We went to Disneyworld for a vacation, and I had so much fun, and I didn't want to leave, but mommy and daddy made me, and now I have to go back home, and it's so cold and yucky."

"I'm sorry to hear that." Nalini glanced outside at the light dusting light dusting of snow coating the tarmac.

"Kendra, come back here." The girl's mother stood up. "Don't bother the nice lady."

"It's all right." Nalini waved at the couple. After scowling briefly, Kendra beamed at Nalini, waved goodbye, and scampered back to her parents.

Nalini watched the family for a few more moments. She barely remembered anything from being Kendra's age, but she did have some happy memories of her childhood. Family trips were a big part of that experience, especially their annual vacations to a different part of the country each year. She didn't know if she'd ever see her parents again, or even just talk to them. Although she'd known they wouldn't take the news well, she'd made the decision to come out to them while preparing for the worst. And, in fact, the worst was exactly what had happened.

She was so glad she'd had Ravi to lean on when she needed help. She decided to text him and give him a quick update.

He responded almost immediately. *Glad to hear you made it to Newark okay, and you have a ride lined up. Does this mean you and Lauren are getting back together?*

Nalini bit her lip. *I don't know. I don't want to make any assumptions, but I'll find out when I see her.*

Tell her how you feel about her, he replied. *She needs to know.*

I'm not sure she'll forgive me for leaving her like I did, regardless of my feelings.

Do it anyway. Tell her.

With a sigh, Nalini promised to give Ravi another update after she'd got back to the dorm. She sat staring at her phone for a while.

What if Lauren didn't feel the same way about her? After the whole experience in Mumbai and effectively losing her parents, Nalini didn't want to lose Lauren as well. For now, she was glad Lauren had agreed to meet her in Bangor. That was a good sign. It had to be.

After a while, Nalini debated getting some coffee but finally decided against it. Maybe she could get some rest while she waited for boarding and ask the family across from her if they could wake her when it was time. Just then her stomach rumbled, and she realized it had been a while since her last meal. Somehow, she could never spend more than an hour in an airport without buying something to eat, despite the ridiculously inflated prices. She had plenty of time left, so she slowly got to her feet and walked down the hallway until she came to a map of the terminal. She skipped past the listings for specialty restaurants and located the nearest food court.

When Nalini returned to the gate, she felt a lot better. Kendra's family was still there, and the girl gave her a huge grin when she sat down. Although Nalini was still tired, she didn't think she could sleep, so she returned to the e-book she'd started reading on her flight.

Much to Nalini's relief, the flight into Bangor arrived on time, despite the snow that was falling when they landed. Nalini realized the worst was yet to come, and she felt a flash of guilt at asking Lauren to drive out to Bangor in this weather. The brief surge of adrenaline that had kept her going in Newark after talking to Lauren had faded, leaving her drained of energy once more.

By the time she'd collected her luggage, bundled up, and stepped outside, the storm had picked up its pace. She had texted Lauren a couple of minutes earlier, and she spotted Lauren's Outback through the dense curtain of snowflakes that whipped across her face. As Nalini shuffled toward the car, Lauren jumped out to help with the luggage. Despite the fatigue that had turned her limbs to jelly, Nalini's pulse quickened when she drank in the sight of Lauren's full lips. Lauren's expression lacked its usual warmth, though.

"Change in plans," Lauren said, when they'd got into the car. "The snow started earlier than forecast, and the roads are already a mess. I hope you don't mind, but I think we'd be safer if we just got a hotel room for the night." She peered out the window and pulled away from the curb. "The Sheraton's right here, across from the terminal, but they're pretty expensive. There's a bunch of chain motels along Route 2 after we get out of the airport, and I can just pick the closest one. I'm sure they should have something available, even though it's New Year's Eve."

Nalini nodded, barely able to keep her eyes open now. A warm, soft hotel bed sounded awfully appealing. Frankly, though, rational thought was no longer an option. If Lauren had threatened to tie her up and throw her in the trunk, she probably would have agreed. The motion of the car lulled her into a fitful rest after Lauren merged onto the road toward the terminal exit.

She vaguely realized she was stumbling down the hallway to their room a short while later. She wheeled her luggage into a corner, summoned enough energy to kick off her shoes, and collapsed on the nearer of the two queen beds.

"I love you, Lauren," she whispered, just before sleep claimed her.

TWENTY-EIGHT

AUREN'S HANDS TREMBLED as she gently pulled the covers over Nalini's sleeping form. The heartache she'd felt when Nalini had called early that morning had largely dissipated, but now she was more confused than ever. Had she heard right?

She told herself it didn't matter. Even if Nalini did love her, they could never be together. As much as she hated the thought of Nalini being married, she couldn't bear the burden of sharing her with someone else. That morning, once she'd got past the shock of seeing Nalini's name come up on her phone, she'd almost let the call go to voicemail, afraid that it would hurt too much to hear Nalini's voice again.

Now, although it still hurt, she had to admit she was glad to see Nalini. It had even been worth driving white-knuckled on the last ten minutes or so of her trip to Bangor, with the snow coming down hard and reducing visibility to a few feet. After Nalini had left for India, the physical separation had been too much to bear, as much as she'd tried to convince herself that it would help her forget about what they'd once had.

A part of her didn't want to forget, though. She gazed at Nalini's jet-black, wavy hair that spilled across her pillow. She longed to run her fingers through it, as she'd done so many times before. Nalini began to snore softly, and Lauren suppressed a smile. How was she ever going to get over this beautiful, funny, and smart woman who had stolen her heart?

She checked her phone. It was just after one in the afternoon, and she was starving. The motel wasn't fancy enough to have an onsite restaurant, but Lauren had spotted vending machines in a small room off the lobby. That would have to do. She slipped out of the room, careful not to make too much noise, and took the elevator down. The lobby was empty, apart from a solitary employee behind the desk who wore a bored expression and looked about to fall asleep. Lauren recognized him as the same man who had grudgingly agreed to an early check-in at no additional charge, when she'd explained their plight.

Resigned to dining on a bag of chips, she was pleasantly surprised to find a refrigerated vending machine in addition to one holding the typical collection of snack foods. She stared at an assortment of salads and sandwiches enclosed in clear plastic shells, although the prices made her cringe. With a sigh, she inserted a credit card and made her selections. She debated whether to get something for Nalini, but there was no telling when her jet-lagged companion would awaken. They could always come back later.

Lauren began to feel better after her hunger was sated. Nalini was still asleep. She turned on the TV and muted the sound, then flipped through the channels until she found one playing reruns of sitcoms from the eighties. Just what she needed to distract her from Nalini's presence...so near and yet so far. She pressed the button for closed captioning and settled back in bed.

She was halfway through her fourth episode of *The Facts of Life* when she heard a groan from the bed beside her.

Nalini sat up, rubbing her eyes. "God, I needed that nap." Her eyes widened as she looked at Lauren. "Lauren, we need to talk."

Lauren switched off the TV, some of her earlier hurt dueling with the longing to take Nalini in her arms. "Are you sure? Last I remember, I didn't think we had anything to discuss."

Nalini threw off the covers, swung her feet off the bed, and came over to sit by Lauren. "I'm so sorry for how things turned out, and I'm especially sorry for how I hurt you. It doesn't have to be this way. I understand if you can't forgive me, but please...give me another chance."

"What do you mean? You're going to be married."

"I couldn't go through with it, Lauren." Nalini brushed her fingers against Lauren's cheek, and Lauren shuddered with desire, despite her best attempts to bury her feelings deep down where they would never surface again. "I'm not getting married. I love you, and I can't imagine my life without you in it."

"But...your parents?" Lauren was starting to feel light-headed. "What happened? Why did you change your travel plans?"

As Nalini launched into a story of coming out to her parents, canceling the wedding, and being disowned, a tidal wave of conflicting emotions threatened to overwhelm Lauren. Finally hearing that Nalini loved her filled her with warmth, but it hadn't completely wiped away her indecision. Could they set aside the past and start over?

"I don't really know what I'm going to do now." Nalini flopped down on the bed beside Lauren. "I have to figure out how I can pay my dorm fees, for a start."

An idea that had been floating around in the back of Lauren's mind surfaced, and she turned to Nalini. Somehow, it just seemed natural to have Nalini in her bed, even if they were both fully clothed. "I have some news for you, too."

As Lauren caught Nalini up on what had happened while she was away, Nalini snuggled closer. She was genuinely moved by Else's death, even though she'd only met Else a few times. When Lauren revealed her decision to keep the bakery and turn it into a coffee shop, Nalini cheered up and took Lauren into her arms.

"I think that's great," she said, her eyes sparkling. "I can't believe this is happening, but I just know everything will work out. I'm so happy for you."

She pulled Lauren closer still, and their lips met at last. At first, Nalini's kisses were hesitant and tender, but when Lauren moaned and slipped her hands around Nalini's waist, they grew more urgent. Nalini slid her tongue into Lauren's mouth.

They broke apart, both gasping. "I really missed you," Lauren whispered. "And, in case you don't know it already, I love you, too. I've known that for some time now, and that's why it hurt so much when you left."

"I'm sorry." Nalini cupped Lauren's face in her hands. "Can you forgive me?"

In response, Lauren kissed Nalini, devouring the lips that she'd been deprived of for so long. "So...will you move in with me?"

"What?" Nalini's eyes opened wide. "Lauren, do you mean that?"

"I do." Lauren stroked Nalini's hand. "Think about it. It would solve your housing problem for now. Of course, we'd be at my mom's house to begin with, but I want to start looking for my own place once I get the bakery up and running." She smiled. "It would be our place then."

With a squeal, Nalini flung her arms around Lauren. "Yes!"

Lauren ran her fingers through Nalini's hair and pulled her in for another kiss. She glanced across the room at the drapes, which were still closed. "I haven't even checked the weather, but I'm pretty sure it's still snowing. You know, earlier this year, I had kind of hoped I'd be spending New Year's Eve with you. I guess I got my wish. It might take a miracle, but I'll see if the front desk can get us some nonalcoholic champagne." She slipped a hand under Nalini's T-shirt. "Come to think of it, there are other things I'd like to do first."

With a giggle, Nalini gently moved Lauren's hand away. "Believe me, I'd really like to make up for lost time, too. But after spending almost a whole day on planes and in airports, I could definitely use a shower." She eyed Lauren, a sly smile playing across her lips. "Why don't you join me?"

Lauren didn't waste any time. She stripped off her clothes and followed Nalini into the bathroom. Nalini turned the water on, adjusted the temperature, and they stepped into the shower together. Nalini pulled Lauren against her as the water cascaded over them. Lauren sighed, reveling in the skin to skin contact and enjoying the way Nalini's nipples dug into her back.

"I've missed this so much," she said.

"The feeling is entirely mutual." Nalini grabbed the miniature bottle of body wash, squirted some onto her hands, and began massaging it into Lauren's shoulders and breasts. Lauren moaned and arched her back. Soon, her nipples were hard pebbles, and the familiar heat began building between her thighs. She turned around and pressed her soapy breasts against Nalini's.

"I can't wait to start our life together." Lauren slipped a hand between Nalini's thighs. This time, it was Nalini who moaned. Lauren soaped up Nalini's front, taking her time before Nalini turned around. Next, she covered Nalini's back in rich lather, lingering over the delectable curves of her ass.

They rinsed off in each other's arms and did a haphazard job of toweling dry before they tumbled into bed. Lauren straddled Nalini, gazing into the dark depths of Nalini's eyes while she ran her hands over Nalini's torso. She leaned forward and pressed kisses into the skin of Nalini's shoulders and neck. Finally, she moved lower and nuzzled between Nalini's thighs, eliciting a deep-throated moan.

Lauren groaned with longing when she inhaled the scent of Nalini's arousal. As she explored Nalini's folds with her tongue, Nalini gripped her head with both hands. With delicate licks, she tasted Nalini before stabbing at Nalini's entrance, causing Nalini to cry out. Then, she pulled away and kissed the inside of Nalini's thighs.

"Oh fuck, Lauren, you're evil." Nalini's voice was huskier than ever, making Lauren shiver with desire. "You know how much I want you."

"I do." Lauren held back a chuckle. "I want you, too."

Lauren resisted Nalini's pleas for relief for a few moments before her own hunger got the better of her. She returned to the warmth between Nalini's thighs, licking and tasting every inch of gorgeous, tawny skin. Before long, she brought Nalini to the peak of ecstasy as she swirled her tongue around Nalini's clit. Nalini's groans and sighs as she came made Lauren's need even more desperate. She cried out in relief when Nalini flipped her over onto her back at last.

"I love you so much," Nalini said, the hunger in her eyes still evident. "And I never want to stop making love to you." Nalini kissed Lauren's erect nipples, sending waves of pleasure crashing over Lauren's entire body.

"Well, we do have all night." Lauren moaned as Nalini grazed one nipple with her teeth. "What better way to ring in the New Year?"

"I like that plan." Nalini's kisses traveled down Lauren's stomach and set off sparks along her thighs. Lauren spread her legs wider, inviting Nalini to give her what she wanted so badly. For a while, Nalini resisted, driving her to the brink of insanity until, at last, Nalini's lips found her core.

Lauren shuddered as Nalini's tongue expertly toyed with her, pushing her closer and closer to the edge. Then Nalini slid two fingers inside Lauren, curling them as she thrust deeper. Lauren squirmed with the sudden rush of pleasure.

"Don't stop." Her muscles clenched around Nalini's fingers. "God, I'm so close."

The combination of Nalini's fingers and tongue made Lauren's legs thrash uncontrollably on the hotel bed. Before long, she arched her back and cried out as the force of her orgasm squeezed all the air from her lungs.

It took a while before Lauren could breathe normally again. She pulled Nalini up for a kiss. "I never want you to go away again," she said, her lips brushing against Nalini's ear.

Nalini squeezed Lauren's hand. "I'm not going anywhere without you."

They spent the better part of the next hour in bed, content to enjoy the shared warmth as they snuggled under the covers. When Lauren finally got up, she peeked out through the drapes.

"It's still snowing."

Nalini chuckled. "I don't know about you, but I'm enjoying the view from here."

Lauren twirled around, affecting a pose. "I guess I should put my clothes back on before I go downstairs. You must be starving, though. Want to come with me? You can get some food from the machines, and I'll see what we can do about finding something for our celebration tonight."

A few minutes later, they returned to the room with an egg salad sandwich and chips for Nalini. The apologetic front desk employee had no access to champagne, nonalcoholic or otherwise, so they settled for two bottles of apple juice, which Lauren stashed away in the mini fridge.

After Nalini had eaten, they returned to bed, ready to watch more eighties sitcoms until it was time to tune into the New Year's Eve celebrations in Times Square. A few breaks from the TV were necessary, though, for leisurely lovemaking that left both of them craving more.

When the countdown started, Lauren put her arms around Nalini.

They kissed at the stroke of midnight, and Lauren sighed with contentment. She was right where she wanted to be, in Nalini's arms.

"Happy New Year," she said, tracing Nalini's lips with one finger.

"Happy New Year," Nalini replied before kissing her again.

Lauren picked up her plastic cup of apple juice and raised it. "Here's to our new life together."

Nalini tapped it with her own. "And no longer being just friends with benefits."

"Wait...we're still friends, aren't we?" Lauren raised her eyebrows.

"Of course, silly. Now, about the benefits part..." Nalini took Lauren's hand and pulled her back onto the bed.

EPILOGUE

NALINI WIPED HER forehead with her sleeve. Winter was a distant memory, and the June heat was making its presence felt. Thankfully, that was the last piece of furniture she'd helped load into Paul's truck.

Earlier, they had filled the spacious trunk of Lauren's Outback and most of Emi's smaller sedan with boxes. Nalini looked over at Lauren, who was standing near her car watching Nalini with a smile. Lauren's shirt was tied off above her waist, exposing a delicious expanse of creamy flesh. As sweaty as they both were, Nalini couldn't resist walking over and giving Lauren a hug.

"This is exciting," she whispered in Lauren's ear, "and I can't wait to celebrate our first night in our very own place."

Lauren's lips brushed against hers. "I like that plan."

Paul stuck his head out from behind a mattress in his truck. "If you two lovebirds are quite finished...is there anything else?"

Emi joined them and helped Paul fasten the tailgate. Nalini had been surprised, and pleased, to see how close the two of them had become over the past few months.

"That should be it," Lauren said. "I'm just going to lock up, and then we'll be on our way."

A few minutes later, the caravan proceeded down River Street with Lauren leading the way. In the passenger seat, Nalini took a deep breath. She couldn't believe this was actually happening. The last six months of her life with Lauren had been better than she'd ever imagined. While she'd enjoyed living in Lauren's childhood home, getting their own place had, in Nalini's mind, taken their relationship to a new level. Living with the woman she loved hadn't erased all the pain of her parents disowning her, but Nalini still held out hope for a reconciliation at some point in the future.

They didn't have far to go. After crossing the river, they turned onto Maple Street in a residential neighborhood that was still within walking distance of both the university and downtown Zachary. With most of the students gone for the summer, the town was quieter than usual. Signing a lease in the summer also meant that Lauren had got a good deal on the rent for the two-bedroom, half-duplex house. For Nalini, it seemed like a palace compared to her dorm room, even after living in Lauren's considerably larger Cape Cod for a semester. She did feel a bit guilty about leaving Michelle all alone, especially after they'd got along so well. However, Michelle had reassured them over and over that she'd be fine, and she sounded like she was actually looking forward to some time by herself.

To Nalini's surprise, when the two graduate students living next door saw what was going on, they came over to introduce themselves and insisted on helping with the move. Still, it took the better part of an hour before everything was unloaded. Then, of course, it was time to order pizza and break out the case of beer that Paul had obligingly stashed away in the refrigerator earlier. He'd even remembered to buy some of Lauren's favorite sparkling water.

By the time everyone left, Nalini and Lauren were both exhausted. Still, when Lauren crawled into bed next to Nalini, an innocent good night kiss turned into more. A lot more.

"I didn't think you had the energy for three orgasms," Nalini said, as she ran her hands down Lauren's back.

Lauren murmured something that Nalini didn't catch, but then she turned over and kissed Nalini. "This feels good. Having our own place at last, I mean."

"It does." Nalini stroked Lauren's hair. "I'm glad the air conditioning works. I'm still sweaty, though, but I'm too lazy to get another shower, so you'll just have to put up with me."

Lauren yawned. "I really don't know what you did to work up a sweat. And, for the record, I love having you in my...our...bed, sweaty or not. Now, I think we both need to get some sleep."

The next morning, Nalini took several long, slow breaths before knocking on the door to her research advisor's office. She'd woken early, in something of a panic at starting this new phase of her career. Thankfully, Lauren had known exactly what to do to relieve some of Nalini's stress.

Dr. Sienna Blake soon set Nalini at ease after discussing her current research projects. Nalini had met her at the graduate student orientation on the first day of classes, and she'd taken an instant liking to the confident and charming woman. She had checked out the Blake laboratory web page before she'd applied to the graduate program, and when she'd discovered she'd be working as a teaching assistant for an undergraduate course that Dr. Blake had taught the previous semester, she'd been ecstatic. Some graduate students took more than a year to select their research advisor, but Nalini had practically made up her mind from day one. The opportunity to start on a summer research project had been a welcome bonus.

After a tour of the laboratory, Dr. Blake left Nalini in the capable hands of Sophie, a senior graduate student whom Nalini had met once before.

"Today's going to be pretty easy, Nalini," Sophie said. "Basically, you get to follow me around this morning and learn some lab techniques. After lunch, we'll get your lab bench set up."

Nalini smiled. "I think I can handle that."

By the end of the day, Nalini's head felt like it would explode with all the new information she was absorbing, but she was happy. She was learning experimental methods that she'd only read about before, and Sophie was a good mentor. So far, she'd been extremely patient with Nalini, giving her a few inside tips about how to get the best results from various laboratory procedures.

When Nalini had set up a denaturing polyacrylamide gel to analyze a microbial protein extract and shown Sophie the results before winding down for the day, Sophie had been effusive with her praise. It had only been one day, but Nalini already felt like she belonged here. This would be her life for at least the next five years.

On the walk to her new home with Lauren, Nalini wondered what the future would hold after she finished her graduate studies. At some point, she'd have to decide between an academic career and one in a corporate research laboratory. Either way, it seemed unlikely that she'd be able to remain in Zachary.

She shook her head. The future could take care of itself. The long, searching kiss she received from Lauren when she stepped into the house was the only thing that mattered, in the present.

* * *

Lauren deepened the kiss, wrapping her arms around Nalini. She sighed as their bodies melted together.

"I didn't think you'd be home," Nalini said, after Lauren finally let her go.

"I wanted to be here after your first day in the lab," Lauren replied. "Chelsea can handle this shift by herself. We don't really get a lot of traffic in the evenings, and we're actually thinking about closing earlier during the week." She gestured toward the dining table. "Dinner is served, with a little help from Tony."

Nalini demonstrated her appreciation by kissing Lauren again before they sat down at the table. "This is perfect." She glanced at the enormous bowl of salad and lifted the lid on the cardboard box that sat next to it. "Aren't you going to have some pizza, too?"

Lauren took a seat across from Nalini. "I thought I'd try the veggie special, for a change. You've inspired me to cut back on my meat consumption."

"Well, I'm glad I can be a good influence." Nalini reached across the table and caressed Lauren's cheek. "Now that you mention it, I've actually been drinking a lot less since we moved in together."

"I noticed." Lauren scooped some salad onto her plate and doused it liberally with Italian dressing.

They made short work of the meal, and Lauren put the dishes in the sink. She'd been looking forward to spending a quiet evening with Nalini all day. After the dust from the renovation of the bakery had settled and she'd reopened Fleischmann's as a coffee shop, thanks to Chelsea's help, life had been even more hectic than she'd imagined. Now, things were finally slowing down. She had managed to hire part-time help, which would be even more important once she started classes in the fall.

"I almost forgot," Lauren said, wiping her hands on a dish towel. "I have dessert, too."

Nalini ran her tongue over her lips and stared at Lauren. "I would love to try dessert."

Lauren picked up a brown paper bag from a corner of the kitchen counter and placed it in front of Nalini. "This is Chelsea's first original creation. She's been wanting to try out her own recipes for a while, now that she's run through most of Else's. It was probably better fresh from the oven this morning, but let me know what you think."

Nalini opened the bag and sniffed it. "It smells heavenly. What is it?"

"Cranberry pecan scones. I think you'll enjoy them."

Nalini broke off a piece and chewed it with her eyes closed. "Lauren, this is amazing. Please tell Chelsea I think she's a great baker. She should try out more of her own recipes."

Lauren took the piece of scone that Nalini handed her. "I know. She really seems to enjoy the whole baking routine, and she's great with the customers. Jen's happy that everything worked out as well. She was so upset about having to lay off Chelsea at the bookstore."

After finishing the scone, Nalini extracted a promise from Lauren to let her be the first to try any of Chelsea's new creations. She stood up and walked over to Lauren.

"Thank you." Nalini's breath was hot on Lauren's ear as they embraced. "I'm so lucky I have you."

Lauren smiled and then sighed as Nalini nibbled on her earlobe. "You are." She yelped when Nalini smacked her arm.

"By the way, I have something for you, too." Nalini's voice dropped lower, sending a shiver of desire through Lauren's body. "It's my turn to offer you dessert. I've been thinking about it all through dinner."

When she'd approached the gorgeous stranger who'd walked into the bookstore almost a year earlier, Lauren had no idea that her life would change forever. She was now the owner of a successful, growing business, she'd be starting college classes in the fall, and she was sharing a house with the woman she loved. She'd even completed several chapters of her first urban fantasy novel. It seemed odd, but now that she was busier than ever, she was actually more motivated to work on her novel.

As Nalini led her to the bedroom, Lauren realized she'd never been happier. Despite the differences in their backgrounds, their two worlds had become one at last, and Lauren looked forward to whatever the future might bring.

ABOUT THE AUTHOR

Arya Collins has been writing ever since she was able to reach a keyboard. She enjoys writing and reading a variety of genres. *Cultural Differences* is her first lesbian romance novel.

Independent authors always appreciate reviews! If you have a few moments, please consider leaving a brief review and letting other readers know what you thought of this book. Thank you.

Printed in Great Britain
by Amazon

23021122R00111